STONE ARCH BOOKS
A CAPSTONE IMPRINT

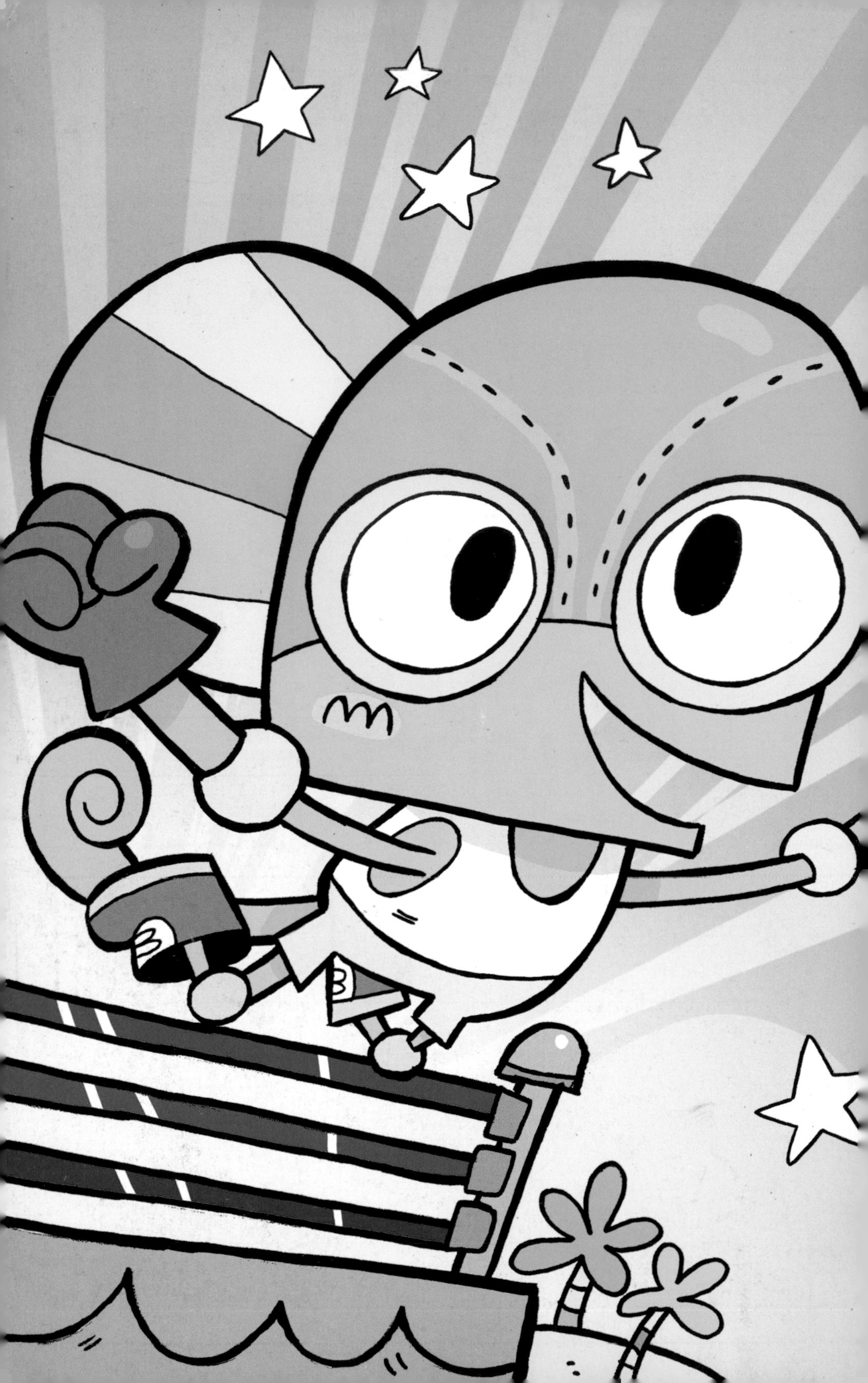

LUCHA LIZARDS

CHAMELEON CAGE MATCH!

WRITTEN BY
DONALD LEMKE

ILLUSTRATED BY
CHRIS "ELIO" ELIOPOULOS

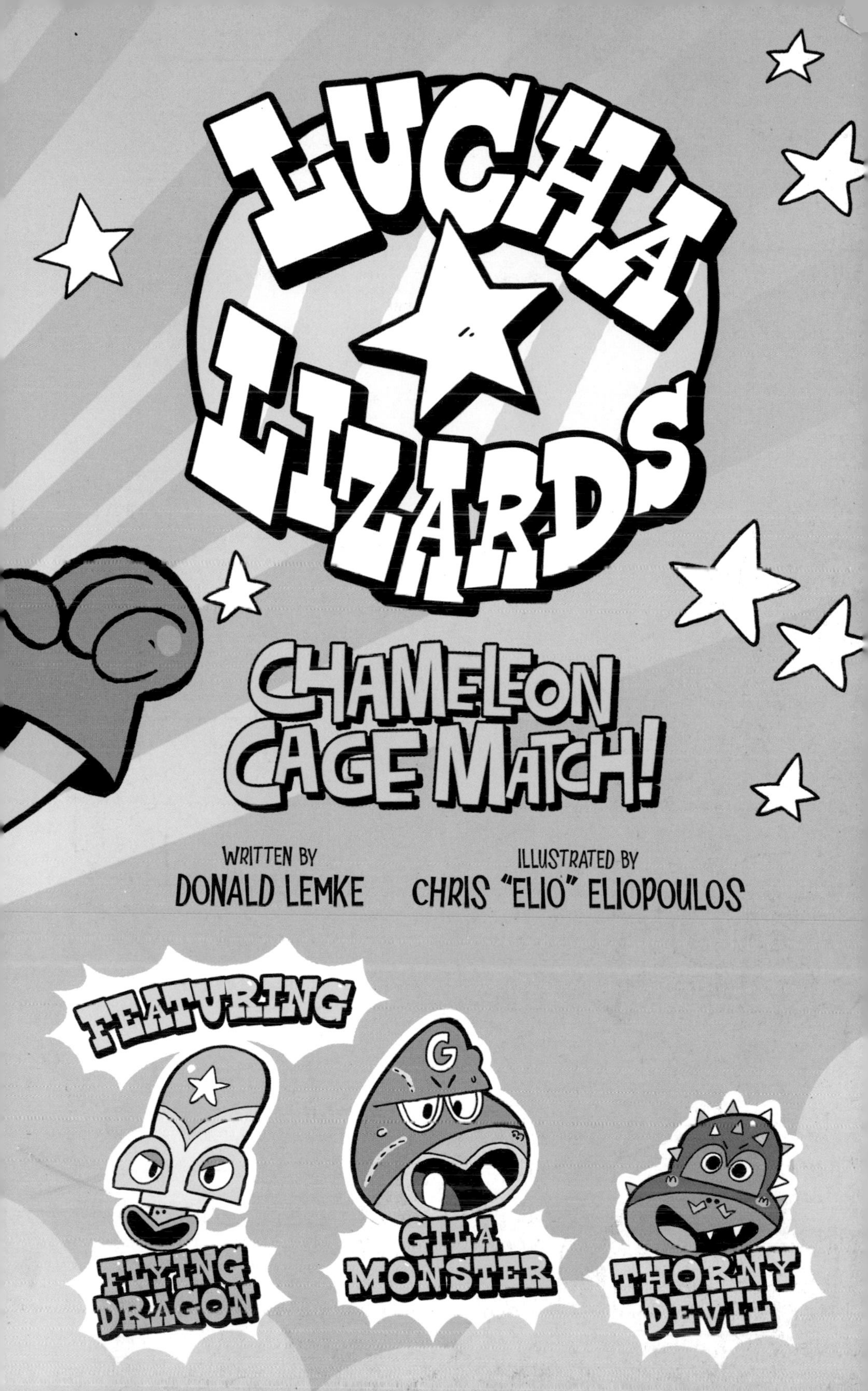
FEATURING
FLYING DRAGON
GILA MONSTER
THORNY DEVIL

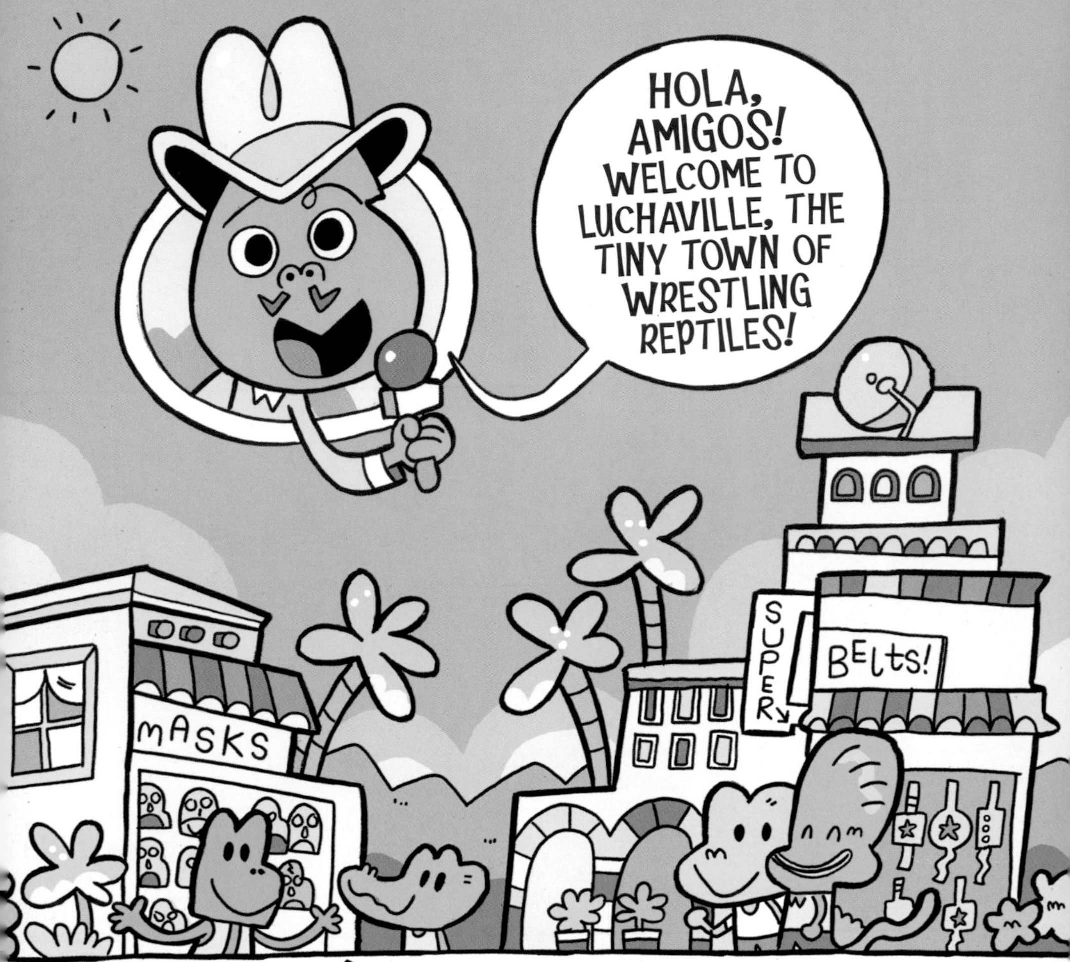
HOLA, AMIGOS! WELCOME TO LUCHAVILLE, THE TINY TOWN OF WRESTLING REPTILES!
MASKS
SUPER
BELTS!

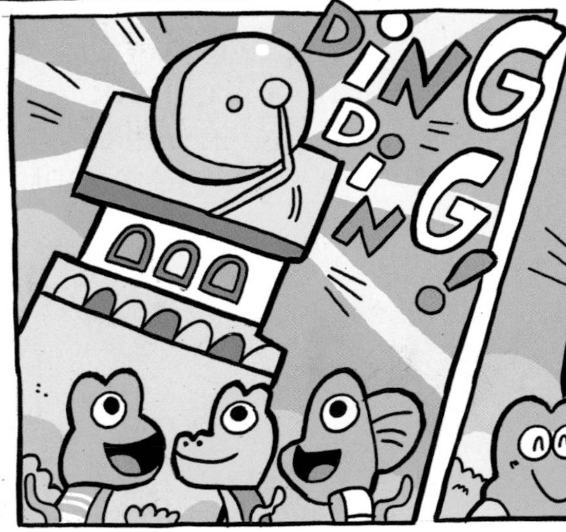
DING DING DING!

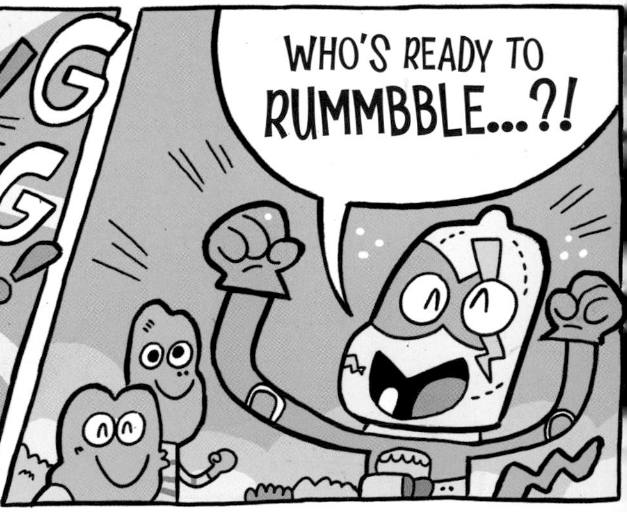
WHO'S READY TO RUMMBBLE...?!

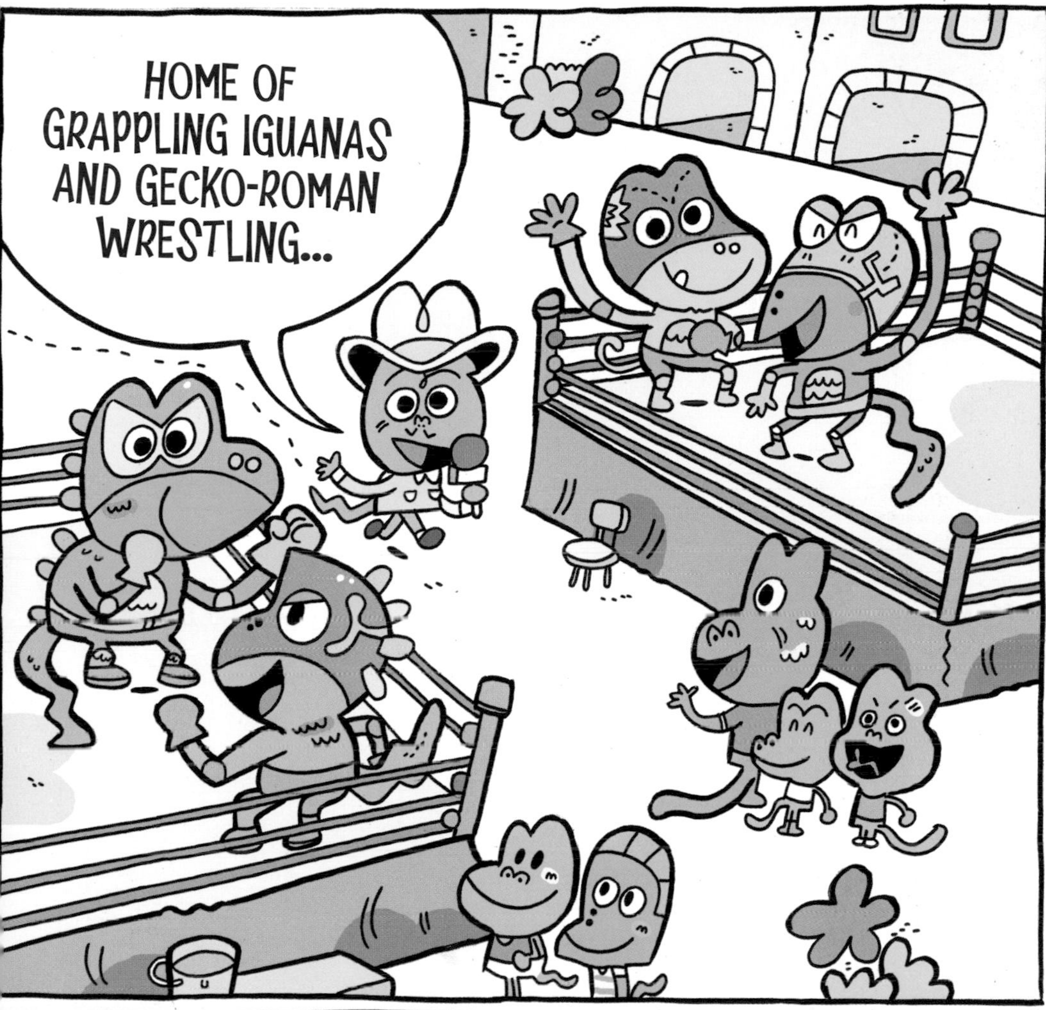
HOME OF GRAPPLING IGUANAS AND GECKO-ROMAN WRESTLING...

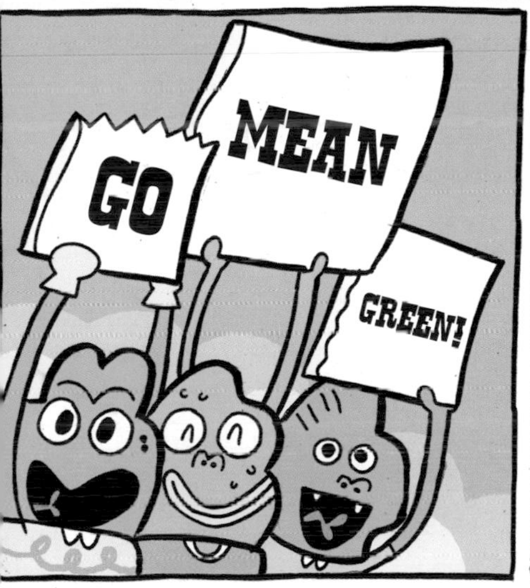
GO
MEAN
GREEN!

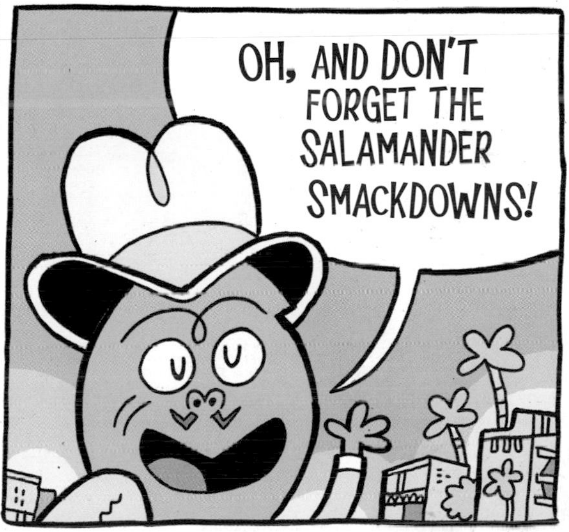
OH, AND DON'T FORGET THE SALAMANDER SMACKDOWNS!

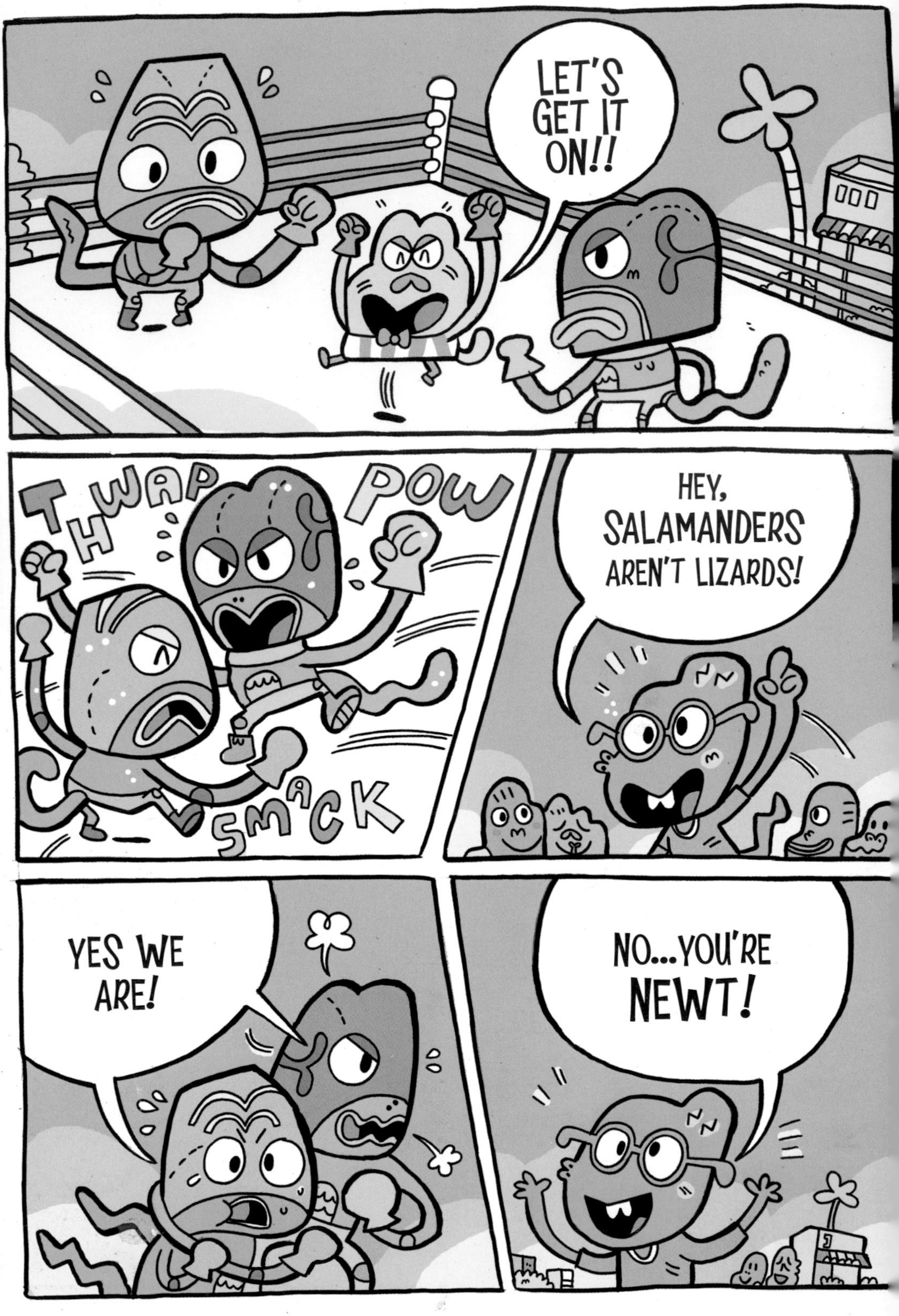
LET'S GET IT ON!!
THWAP
POW
SMACK
HEY, SALAMANDERS AREN'T LIZARDS!
YES WE ARE!
NO...YOU'RE NEWT!

SALAMANDERS (AND NEWTS) ARE AMPHIBIANS... NOT LIZARDS!

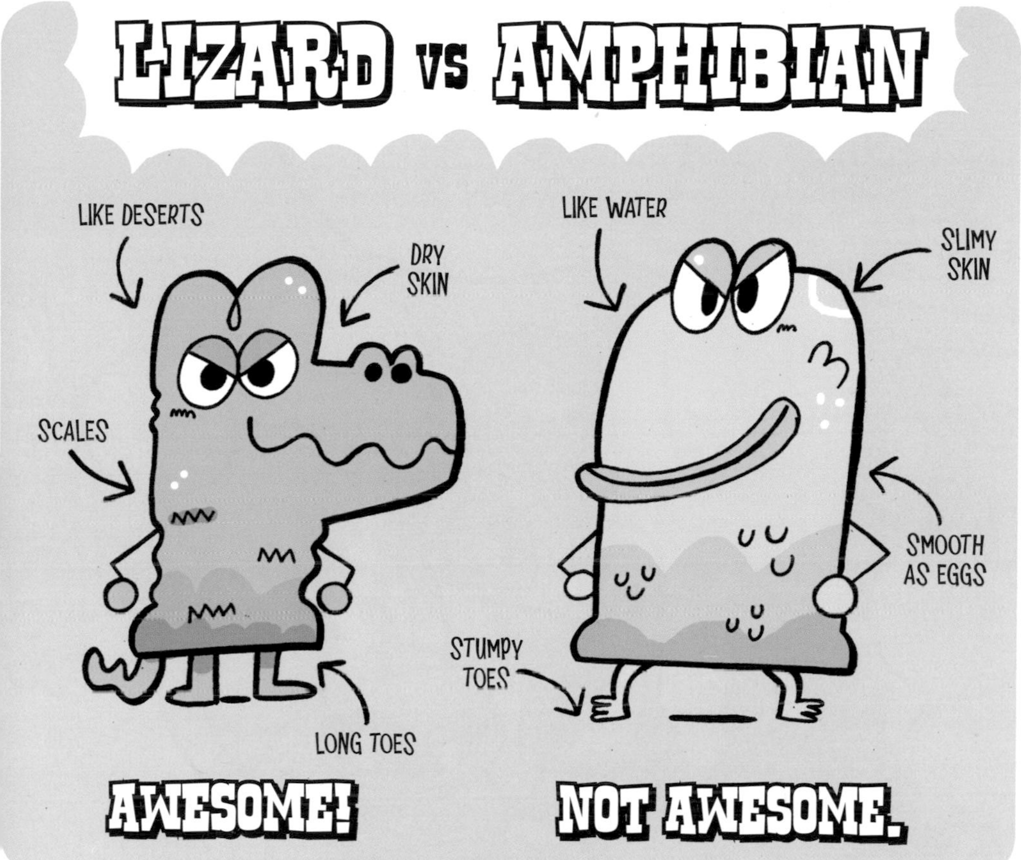

LIZARD vs AMPHIBIAN
LIKE DESERTS
DRY SKIN
SCALES
LONG TOES
LIKE WATER
SLIMY SKIN
SMOOTH AS EGGS
STUMPY TOES
AWESOME!
NOT AWESOME.

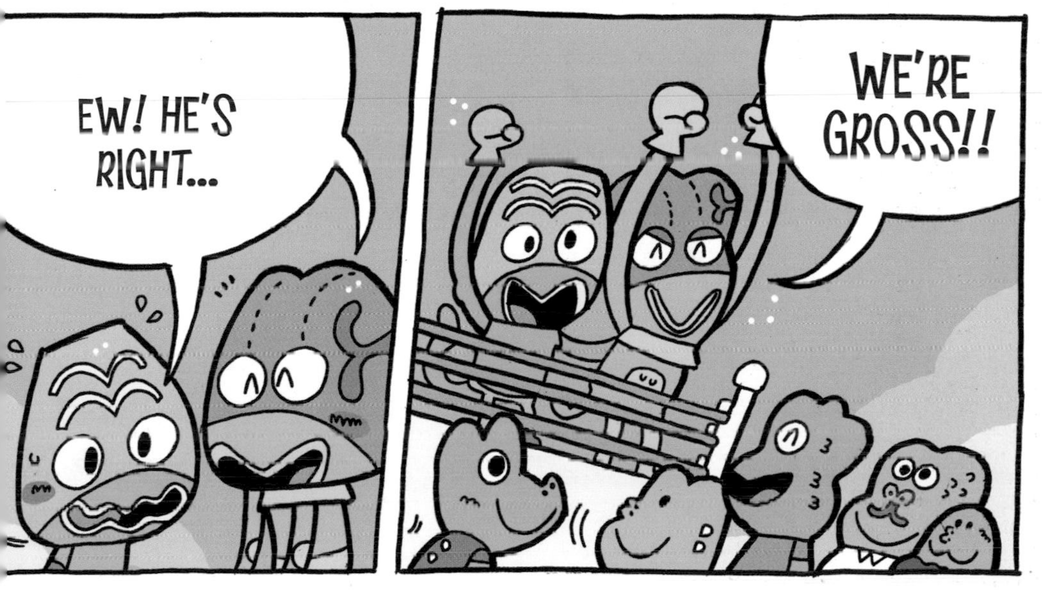

EW! HE'S RIGHT...
WE'RE GROSS!!

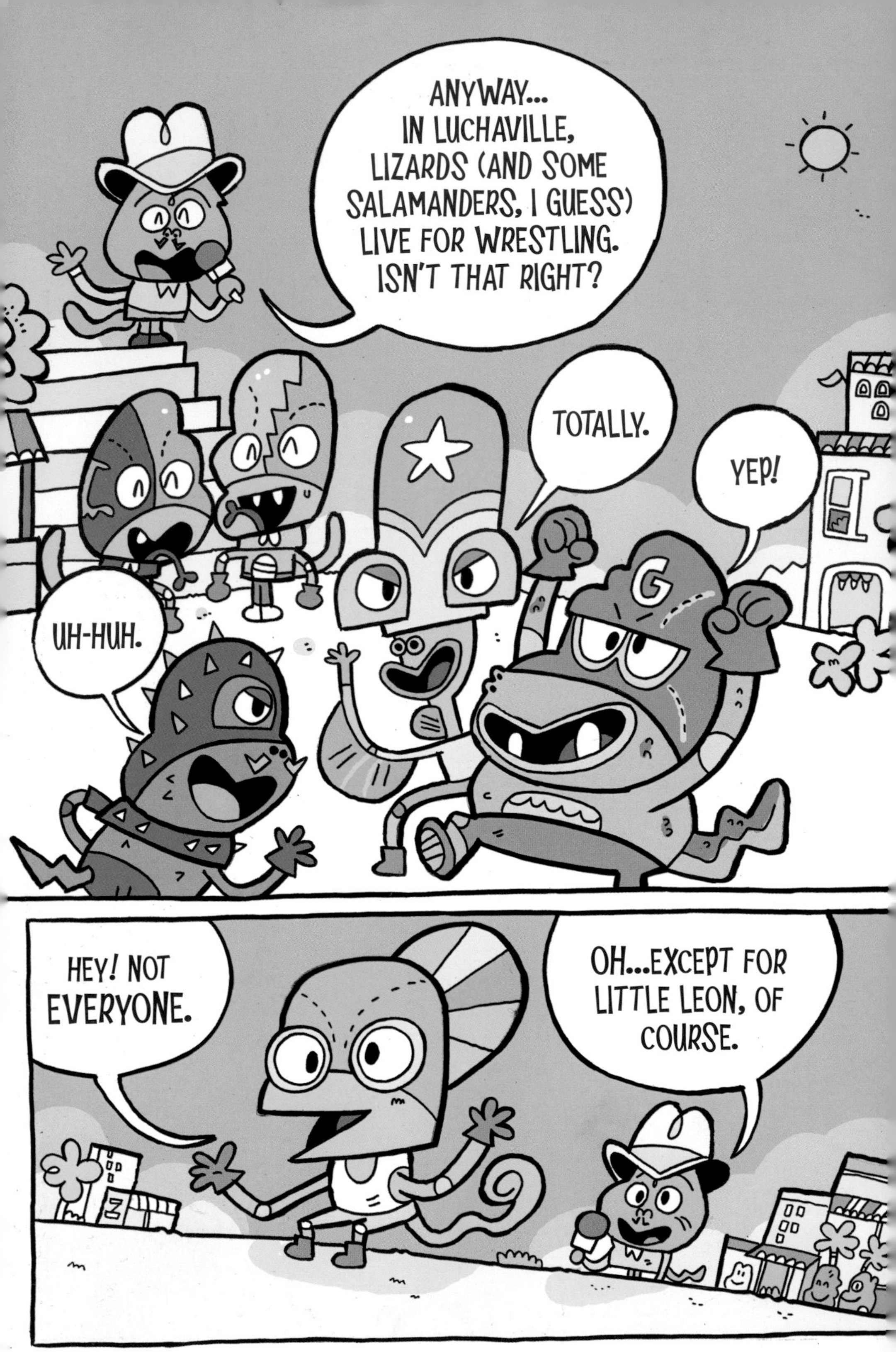
ANYWAY... IN LUCHAVILLE, LIZARDS (AND SOME SALAMANDERS, I GUESS) LIVE FOR WRESTLING. ISN'T THAT RIGHT?
TOTALLY.
YEP!
UH-HUH.
HEY! NOT EVERYONE.
OH...EXCEPT FOR LITTLE LEON, OF COURSE.

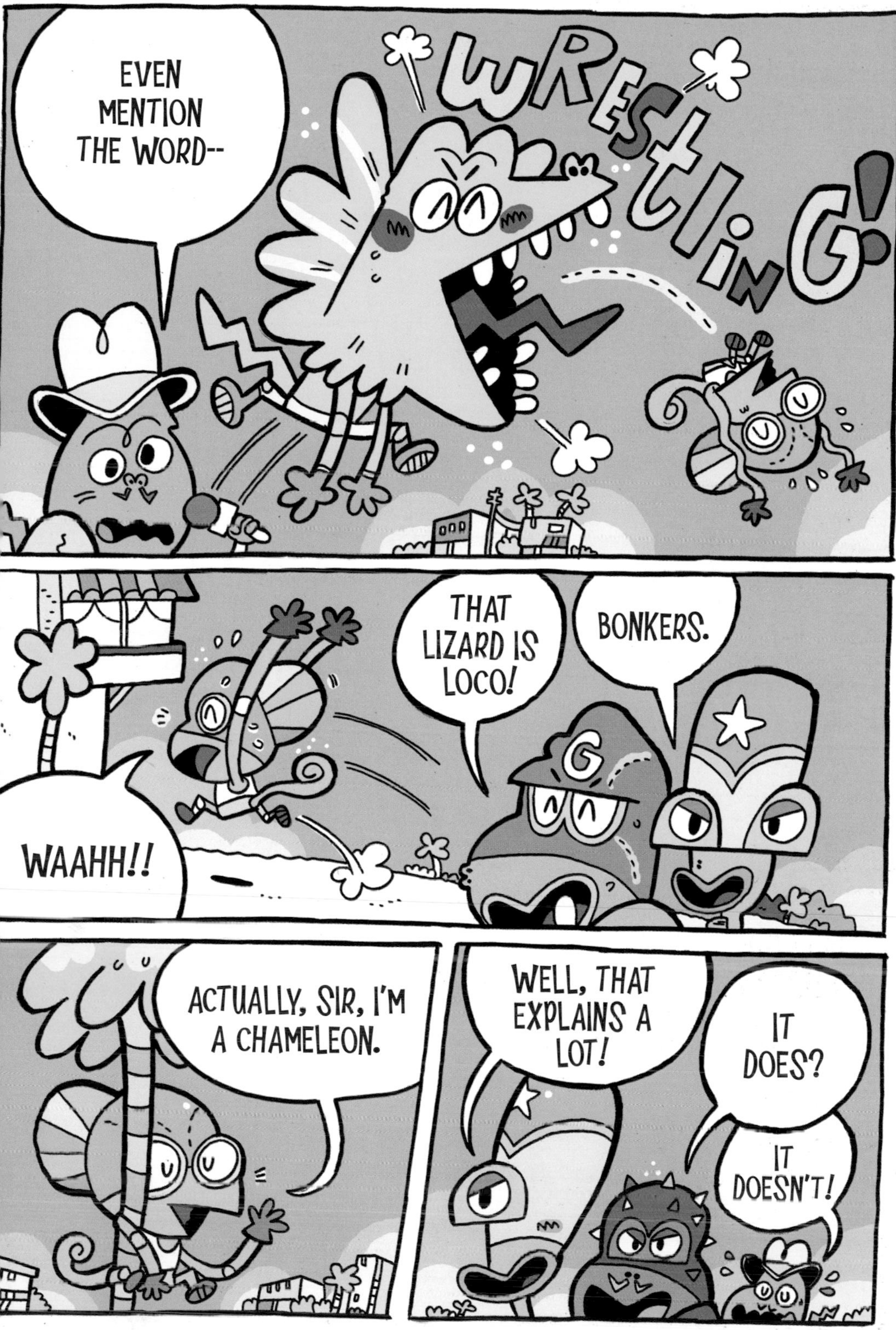
EVEN MENTION THE WORD--
WRESTLING!
THAT LIZARD IS LOCO!
BONKERS.
WAAHH!!
ACTUALLY, SIR, I'M A CHAMELEON.
WELL, THAT EXPLAINS A LOT!
IT DOES?
IT DOESN'T!

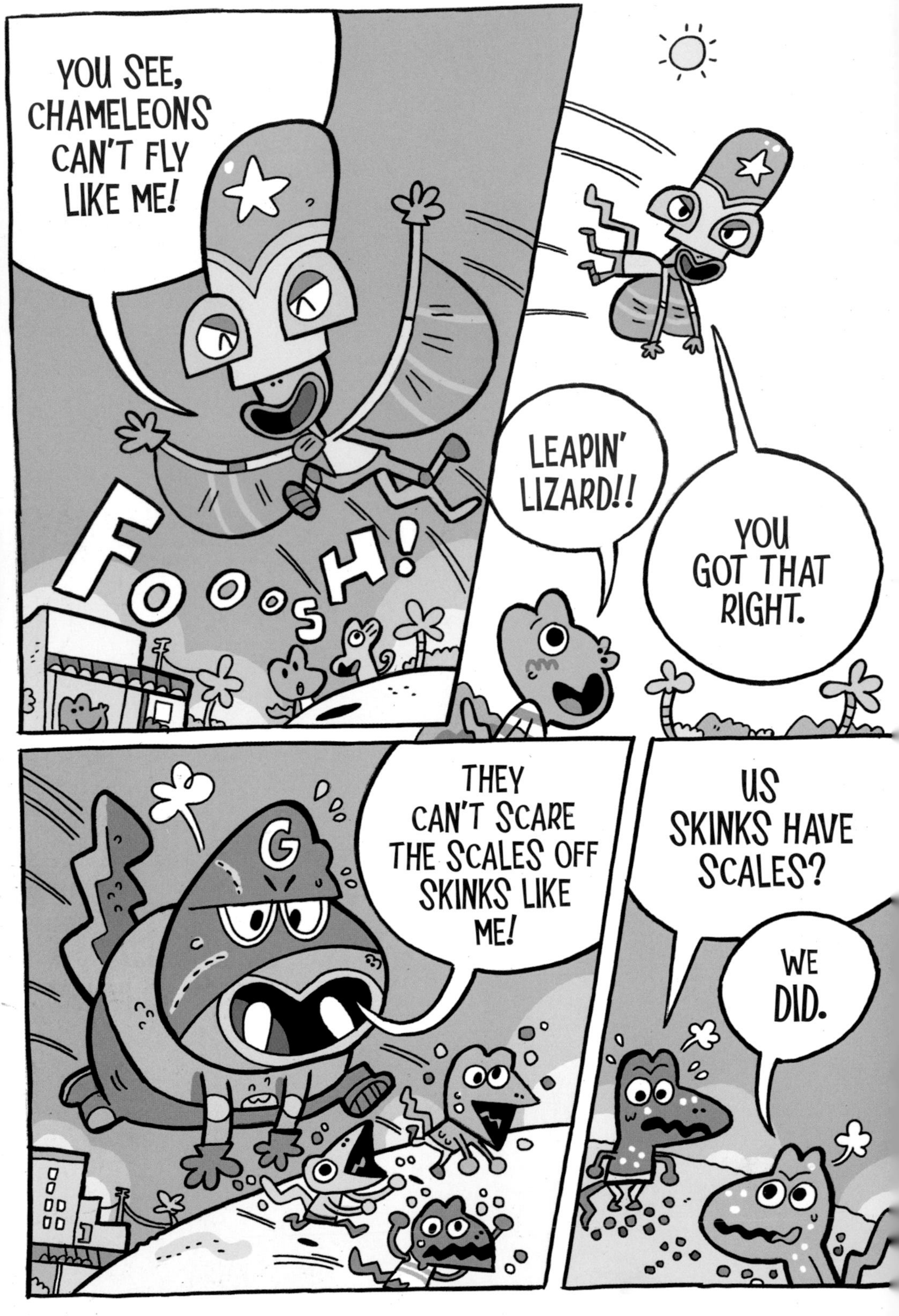
YOU SEE, CHAMELEONS CAN'T FLY LIKE ME!
FOOOSH!
LEAPIN' LIZARD!!
YOU GOT THAT RIGHT.
THEY CAN'T SCARE THE SCALES OFF SKINKS LIKE ME!
US SKINKS HAVE SCALES?
WE DID.

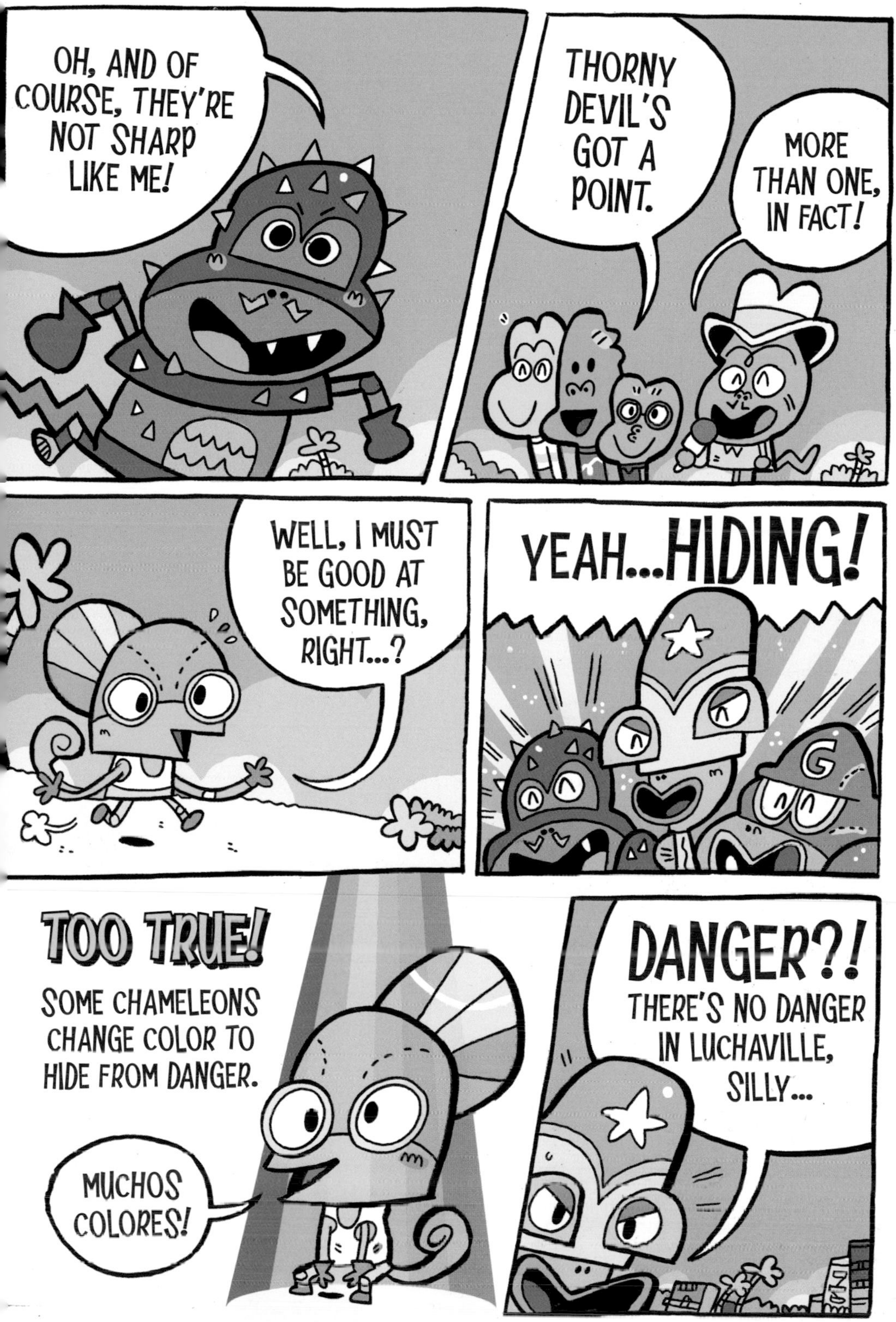
OH, AND OF COURSE, THEY'RE NOT SHARP LIKE ME!
THORNY DEVIL'S GOT A POINT.
MORE THAN ONE, IN FACT!
WELL, I MUST BE GOOD AT SOMETHING, RIGHT...?
YEAH...HIDING!
TOO TRUE!
SOME CHAMELEONS CHANGE COLOR TO HIDE FROM DANGER.
MUCHOS COLORES!
DANGER?!
THERE'S NO DANGER IN LUCHAVILLE, SILLY...

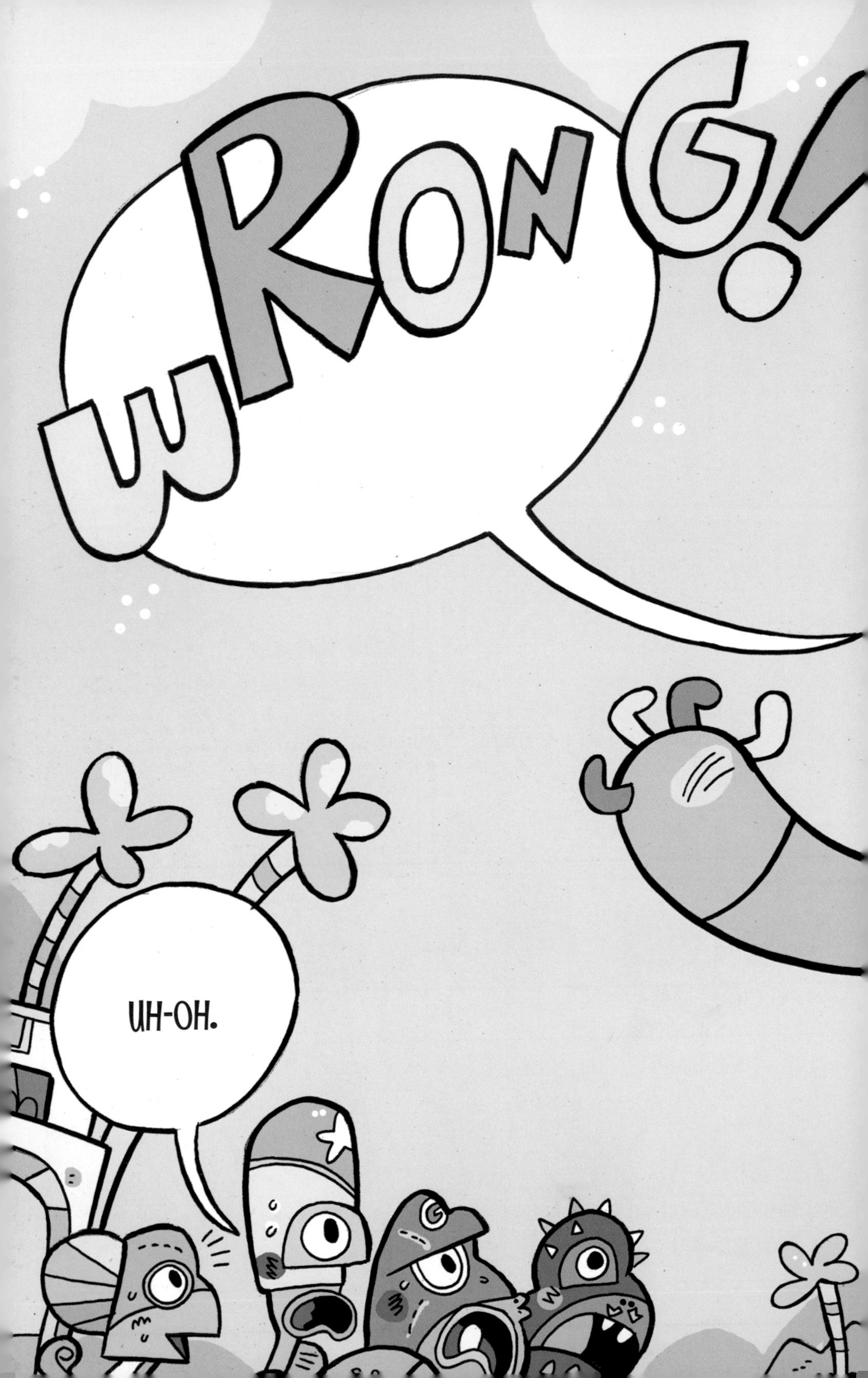
WRONG!
UH-OH.

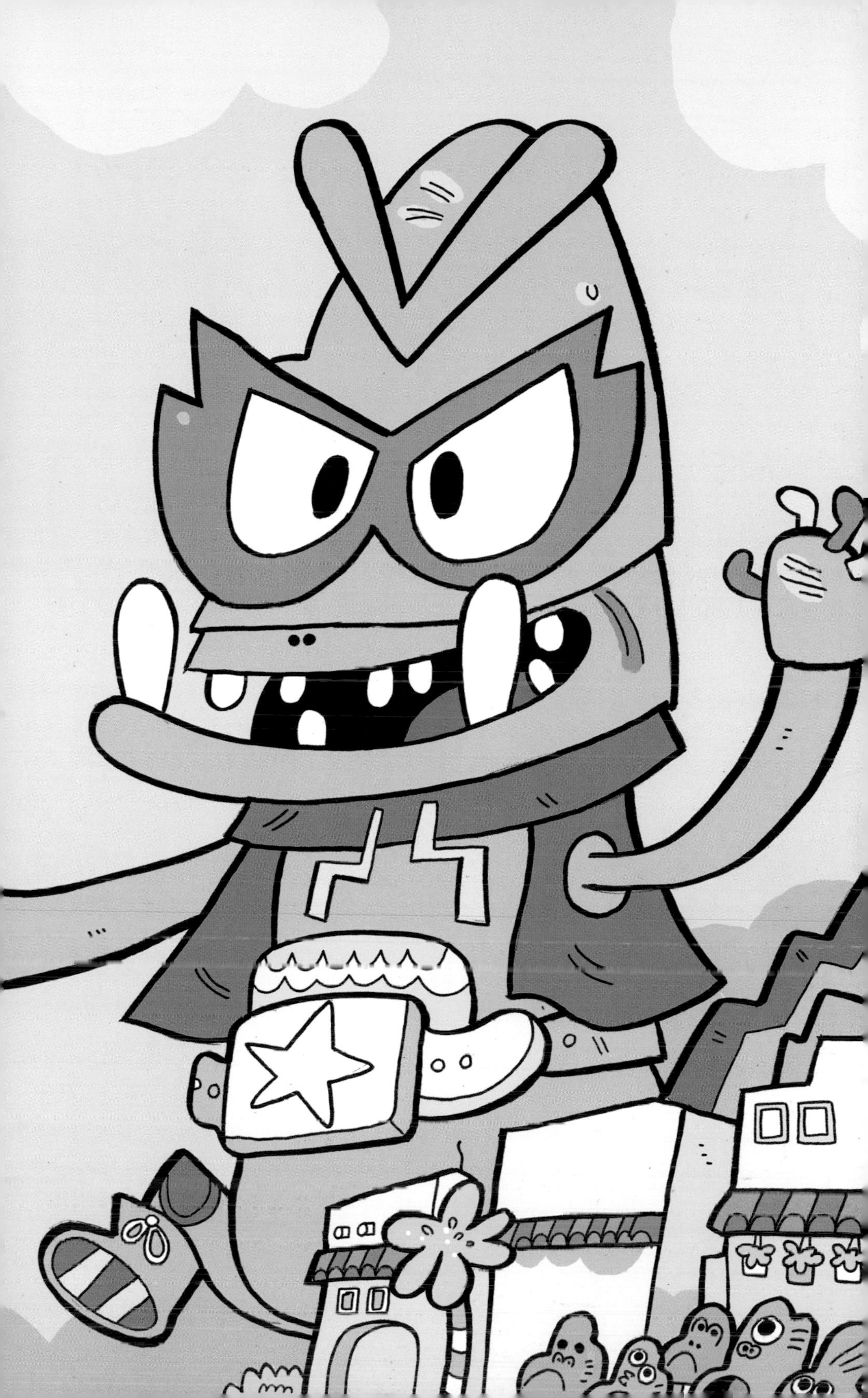

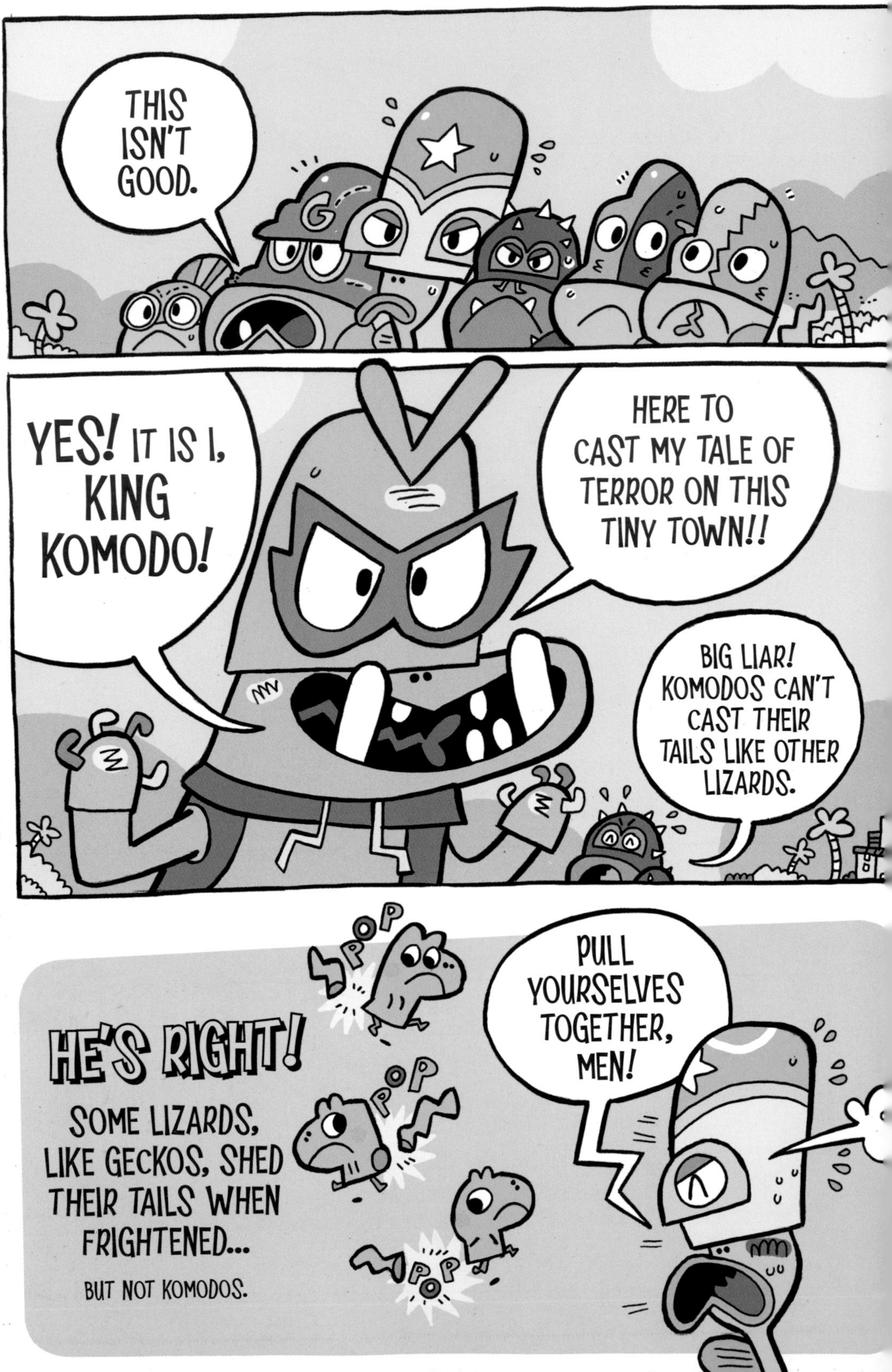

THIS ISN'T GOOD.
YES! IT IS I, KING KOMODO!
HERE TO CAST MY TALE OF TERROR ON THIS TINY TOWN!!
BIG LIAR! KOMODOS CAN'T CAST THEIR TAILS LIKE OTHER LIZARDS.
HE'S RIGHT!
SOME LIZARDS, LIKE GECKOS, SHED THEIR TAILS WHEN FRIGHTENED...
BUT NOT KOMODOS.
POP
POP
POP
PULL YOURSELVES TOGETHER, MEN!

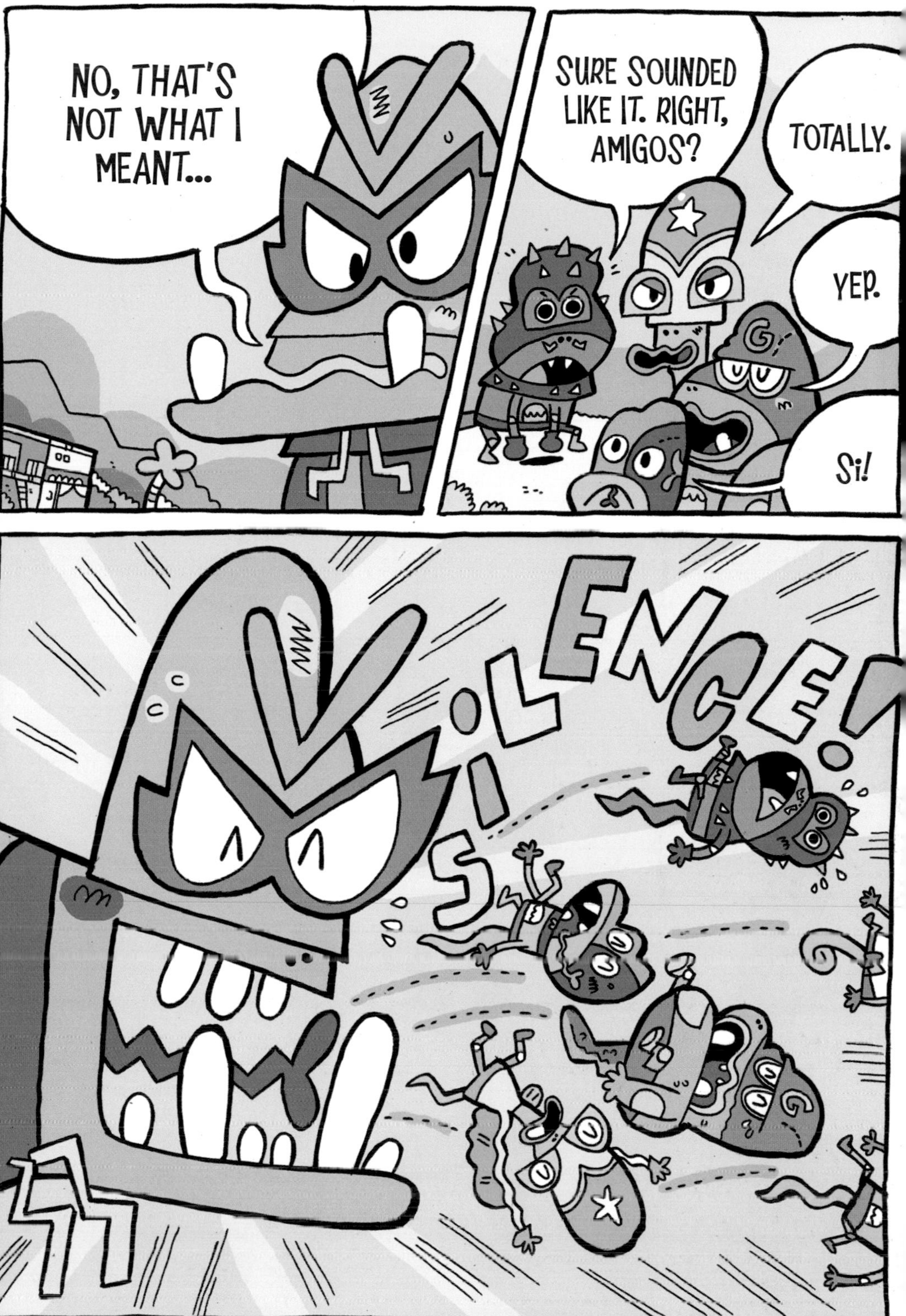
NO, THAT'S NOT WHAT I MEANT...
SURE SOUNDED LIKE IT. RIGHT, AMIGOS?
TOTALLY.
YEP.
Sí!
SILENCE!

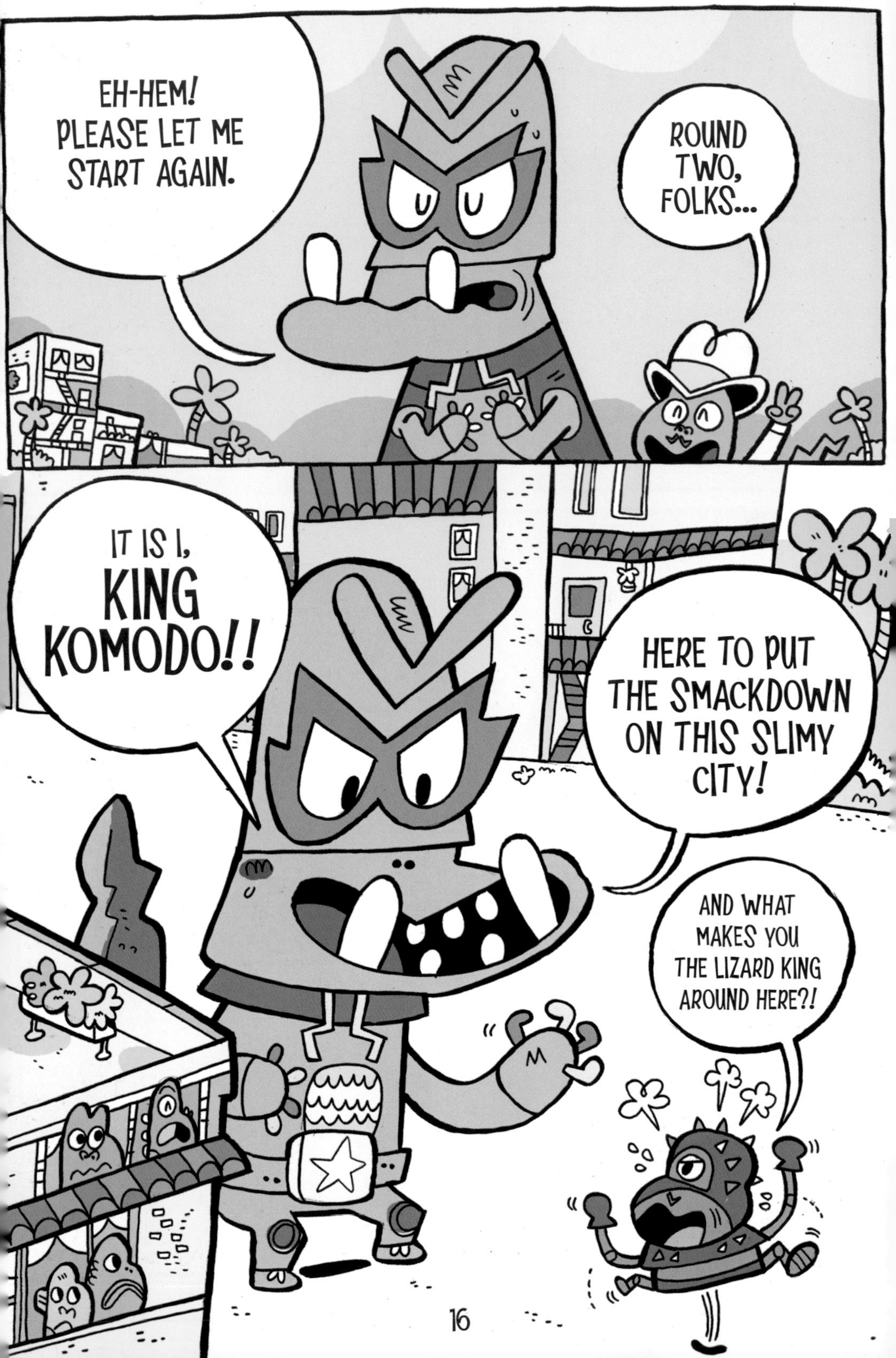
EH-HEM! PLEASE LET ME START AGAIN.
ROUND TWO, FOLKS...
IT IS I, KING KOMODO!!
HERE TO PUT THE SMACKDOWN ON THIS SLIMY CITY!
AND WHAT MAKES YOU THE LIZARD KING AROUND HERE?!

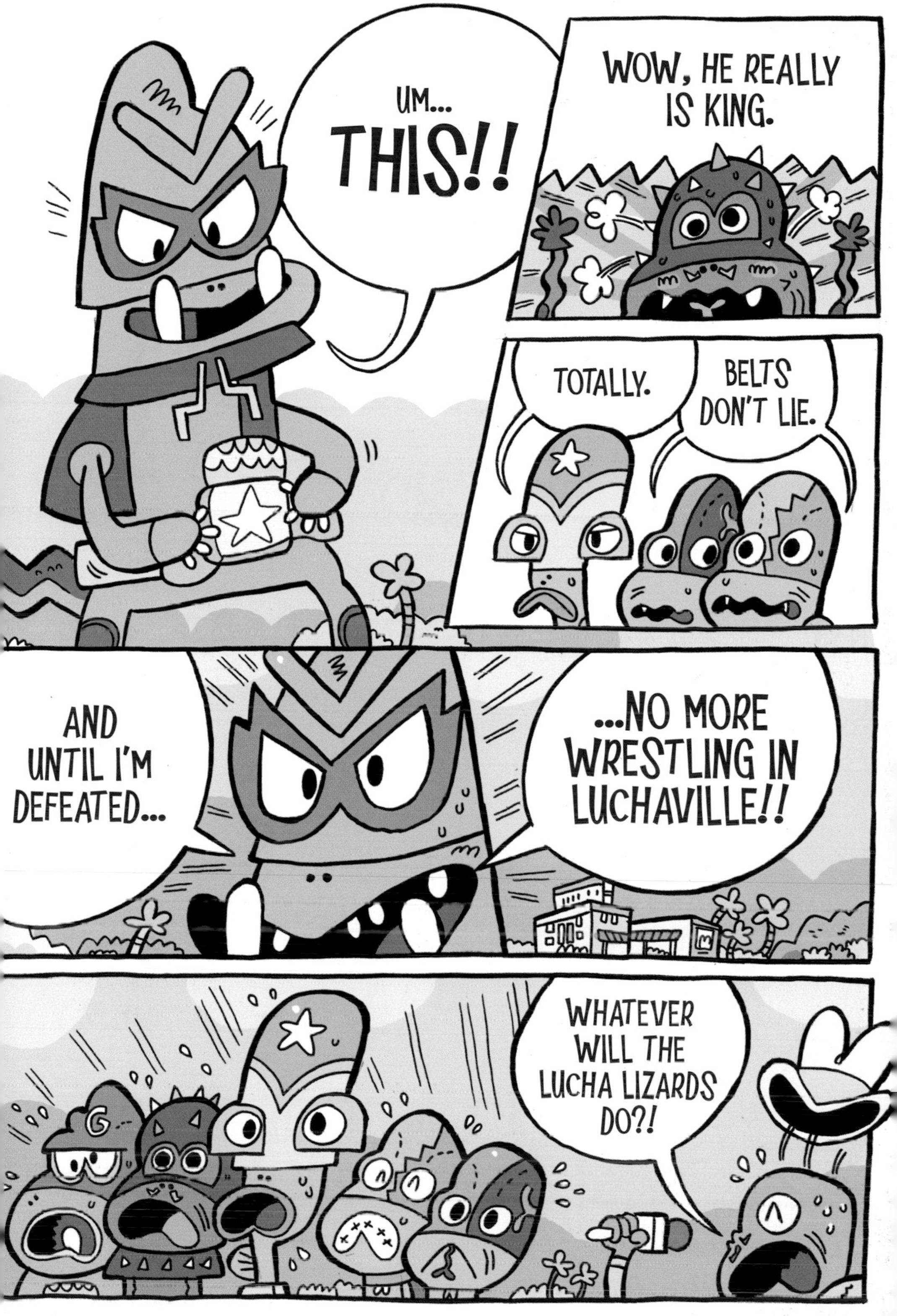
UM...
THIS!!
WOW, HE REALLY IS KING.
TOTALLY.
BELTS DON'T LIE.
AND UNTIL I'M DEFEATED...
...NO MORE WRESTLING IN LUCHAVILLE!!
WHATEVER WILL THE LUCHA LIZARDS DO?!

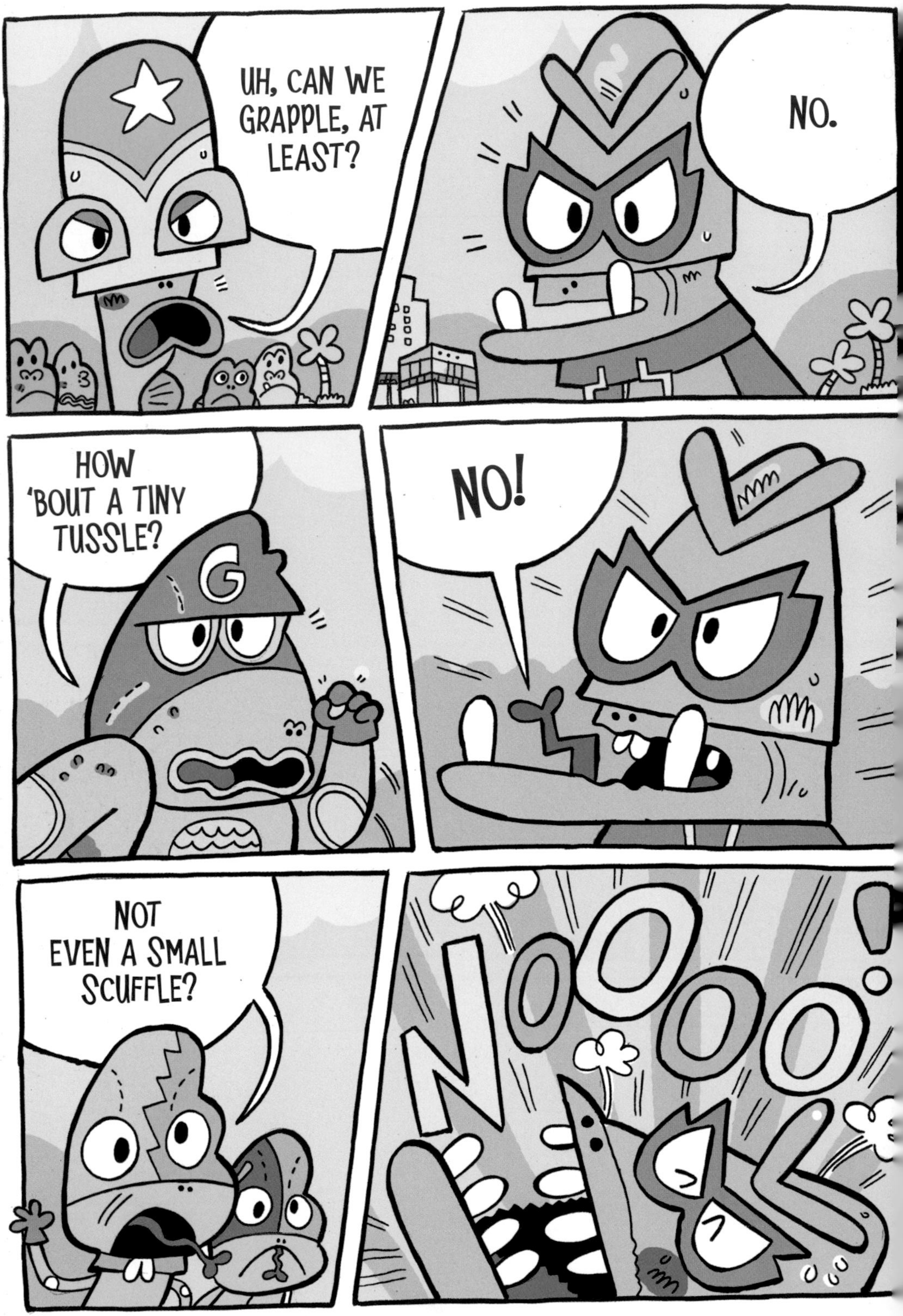
UH, CAN WE GRAPPLE, AT LEAST?
NO.
HOW 'BOUT A TINY TUSSLE?
NO!
NOT EVEN A SMALL SCUFFLE?
NOOOOOO!

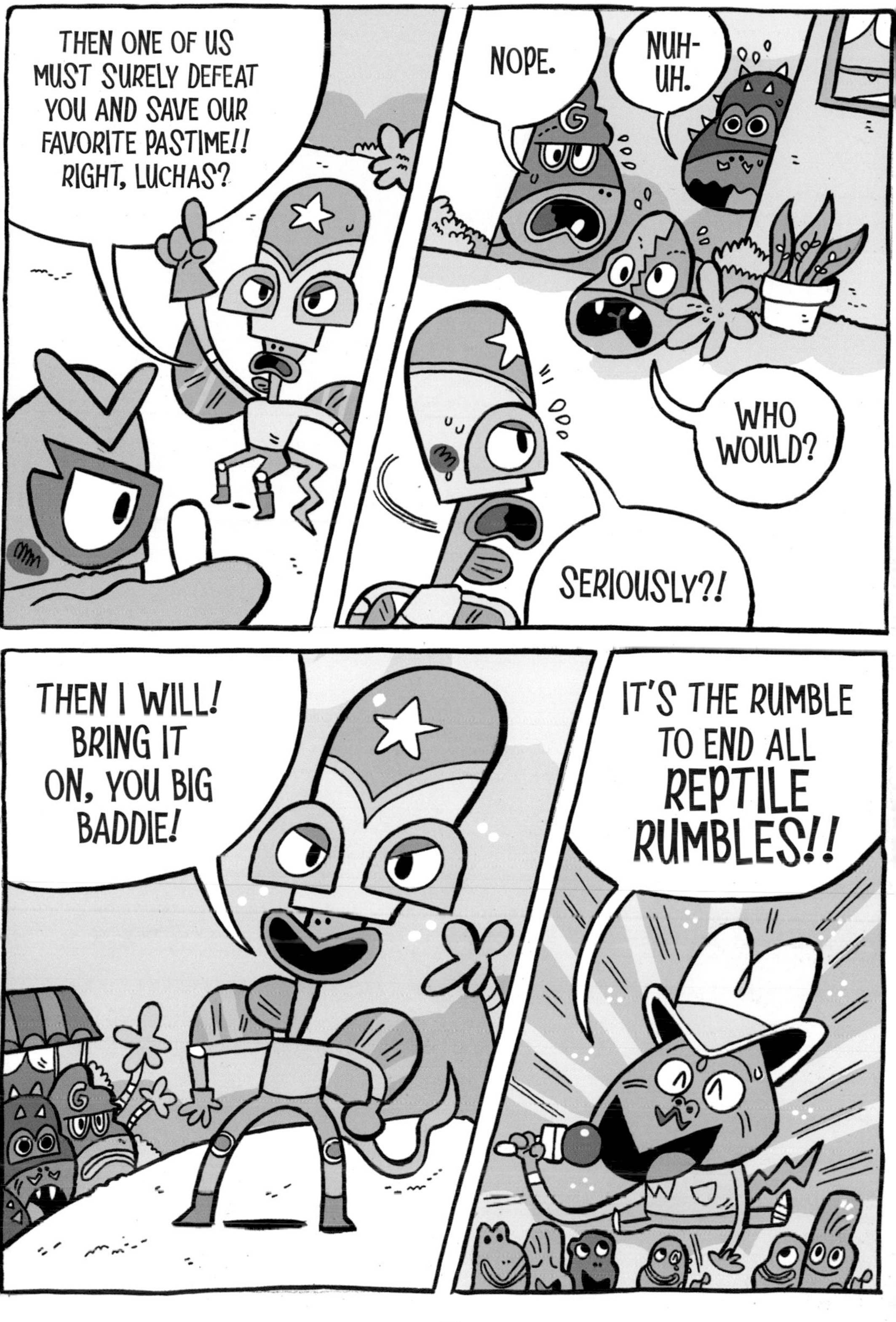
THEN ONE OF US MUST SURELY DEFEAT YOU AND SAVE OUR FAVORITE PASTIME!! RIGHT, LUCHAS?
NOPE.
NUH-UH.
WHO WOULD?
SERIOUSLY?!
THEN I WILL! BRING IT ON, YOU BIG BADDIE!
IT'S THE RUMBLE TO END ALL REPTILE RUMBLES!!

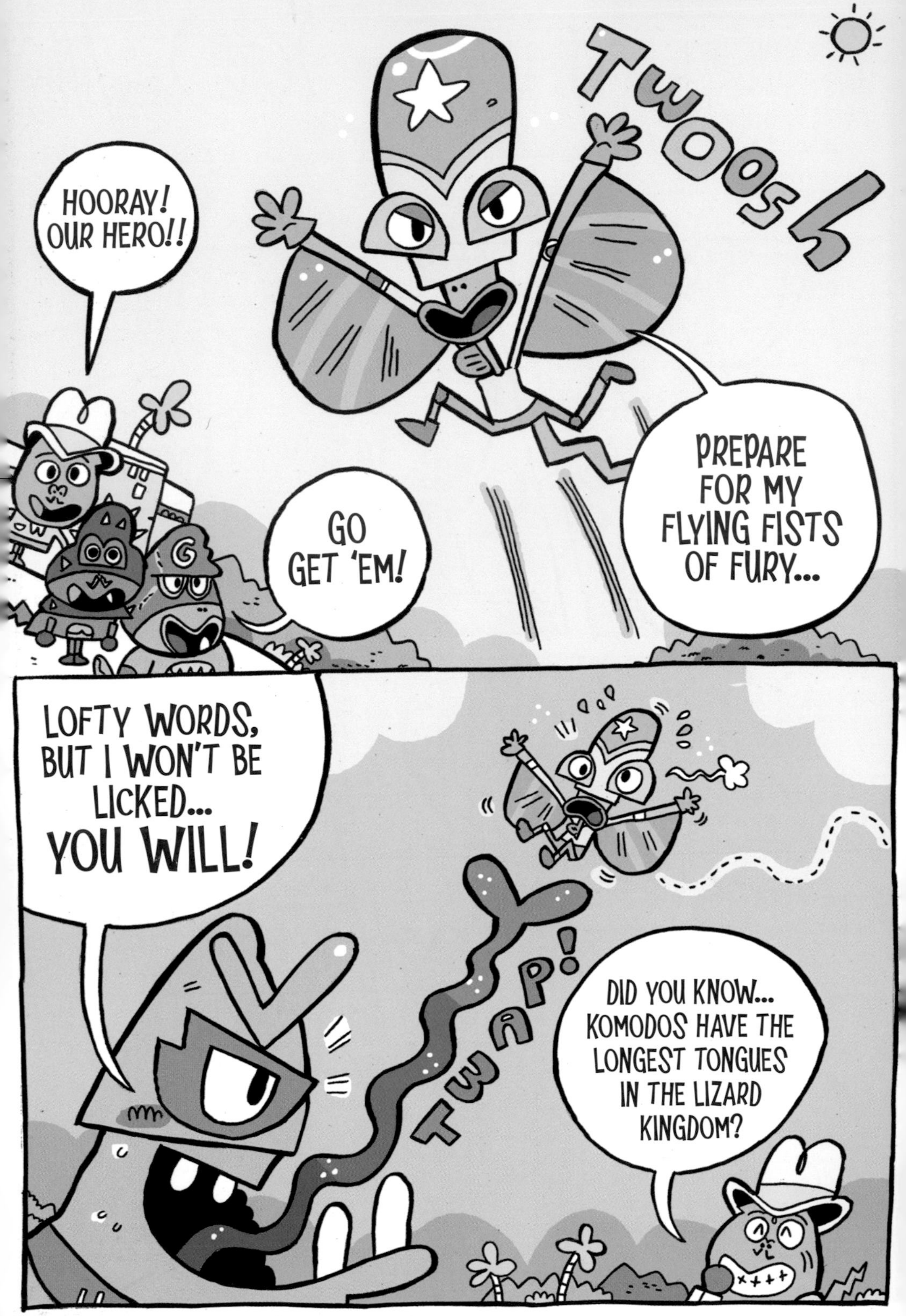

TWOOSH
HOORAY! OUR HERO!!
PREPARE FOR MY FLYING FISTS OF FURY...
GO GET 'EM!
LOFTY WORDS, BUT I WON'T BE LICKED... YOU WILL!
TWAP!
DID YOU KNOW... KOMODOS HAVE THE LONGEST TONGUES IN THE LIZARD KINGDOM?

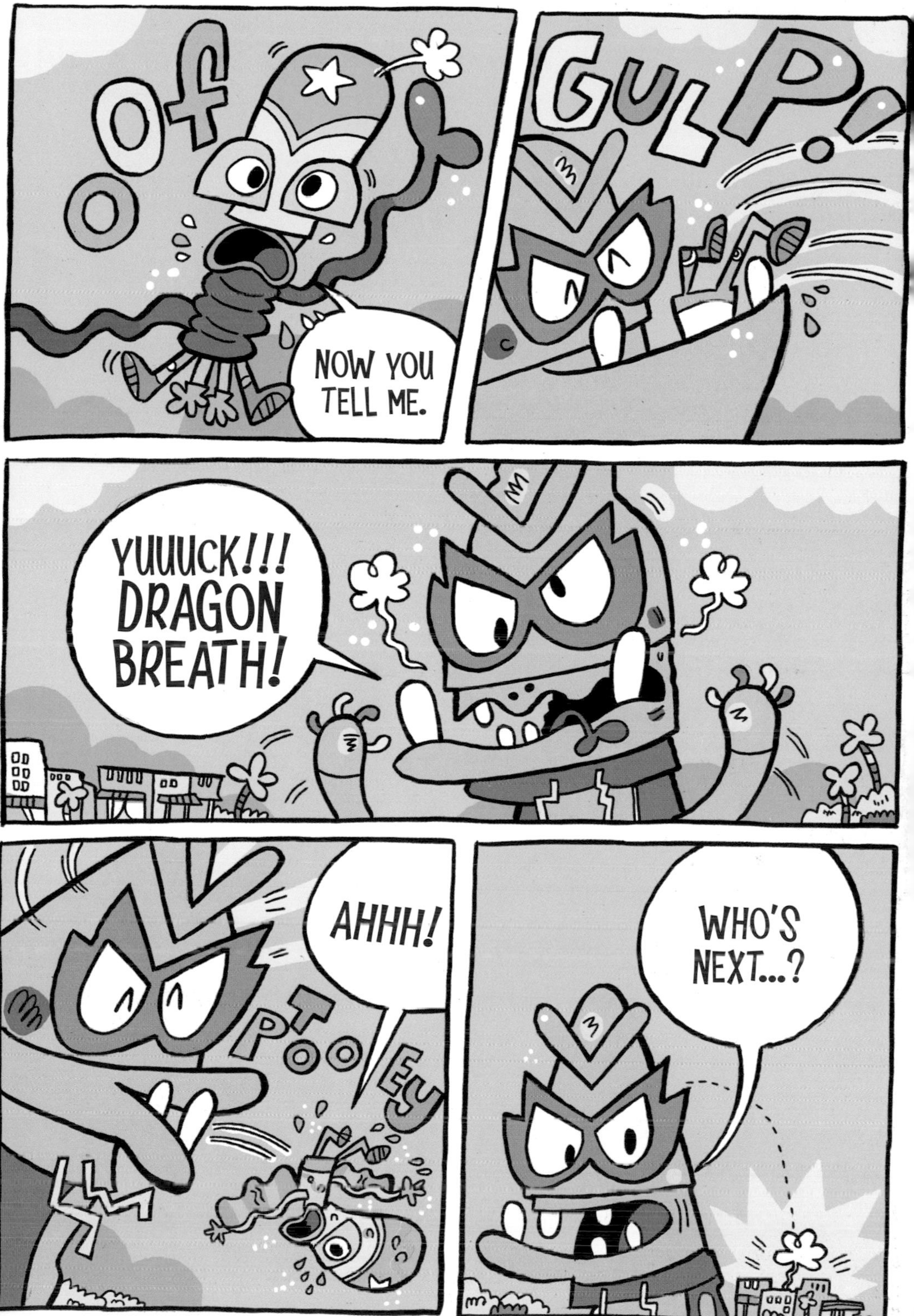
OOOF
NOW YOU TELL ME.
GULP!
YUUUCK!!! DRAGON BREATH!
AHHH!
PTOOEY
WHO'S NEXT...?

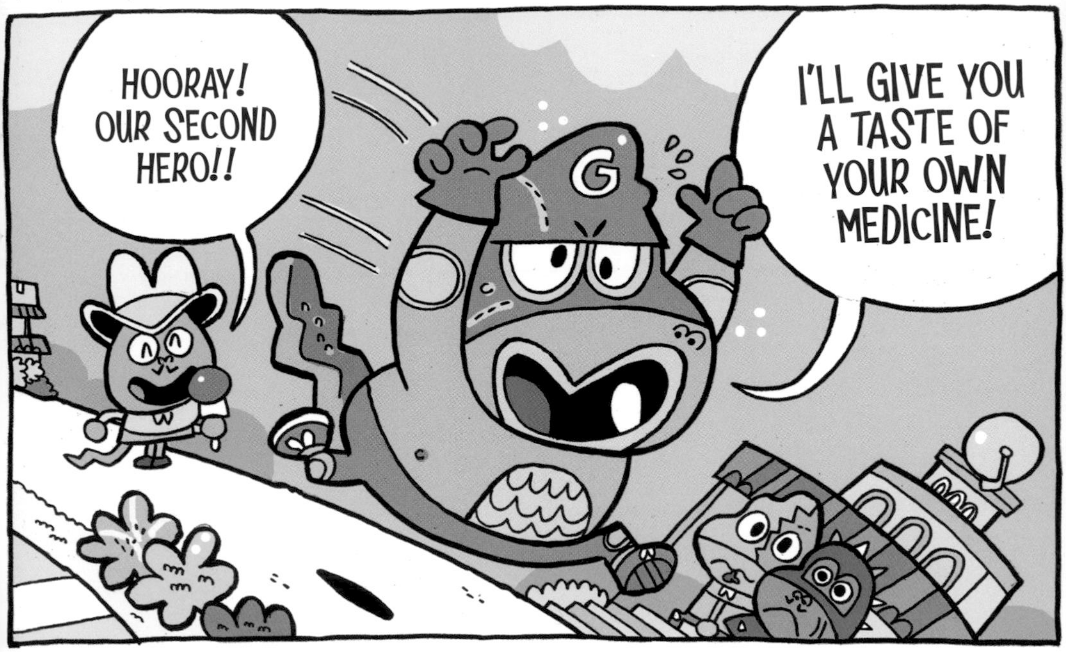
HOORAY! OUR SECOND HERO!!
I'LL GIVE YOU A TASTE OF YOUR OWN MEDICINE!

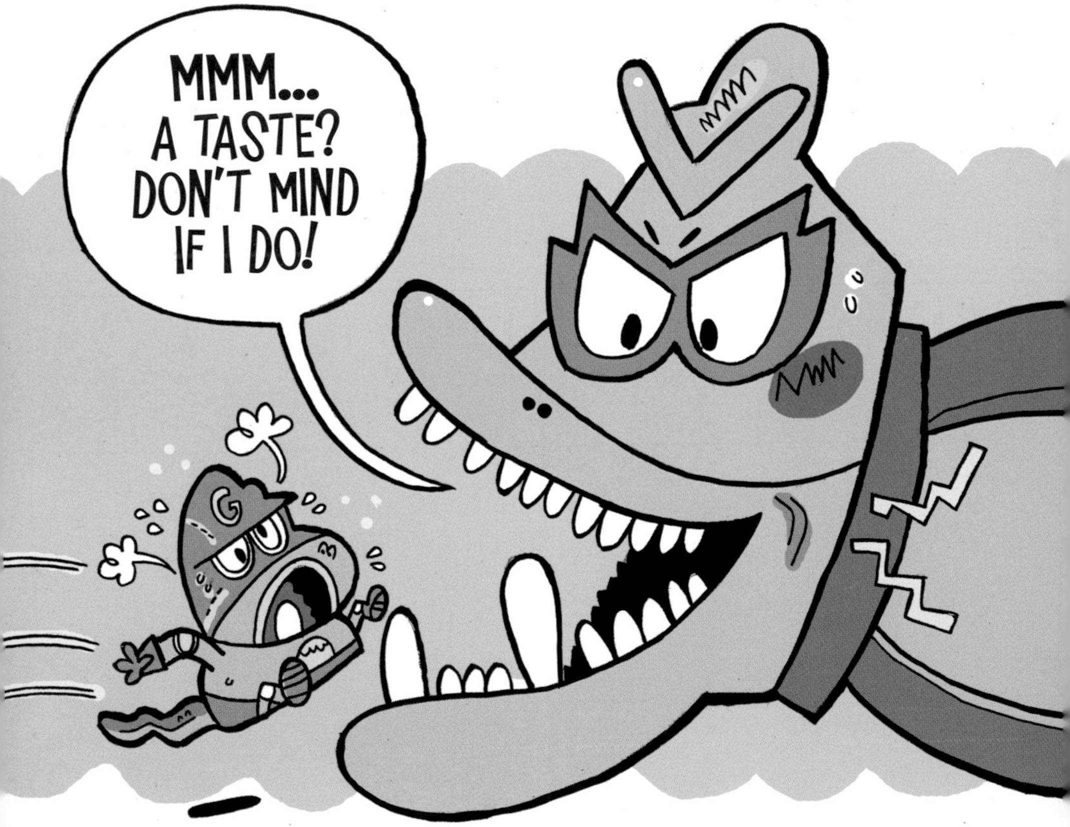
MMM... A TASTE? DON'T MIND IF I DO!

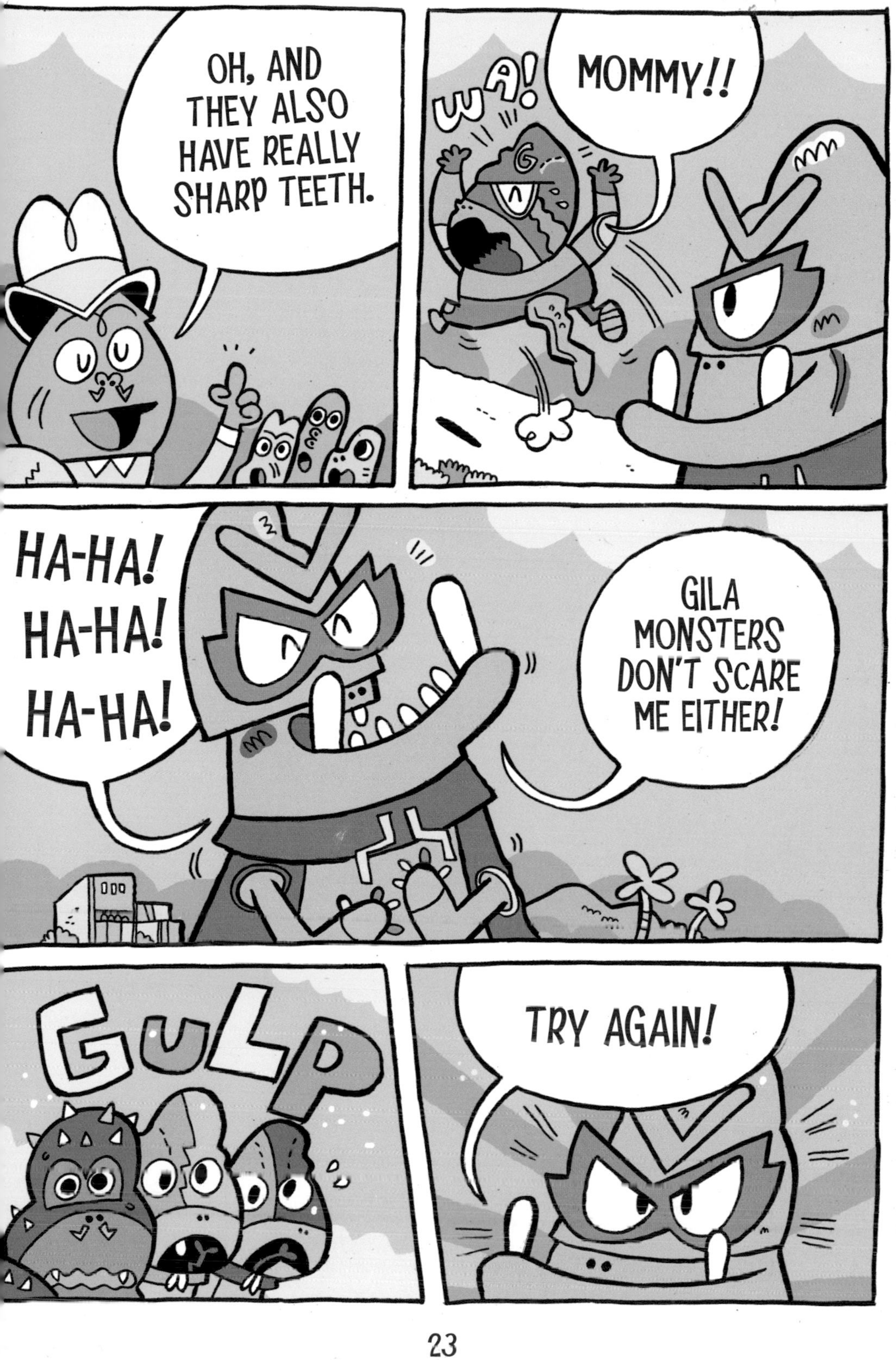
OH, AND THEY ALSO HAVE REALLY SHARP TEETH.
WA!
MOMMY!!
HA-HA! HA-HA! HA-HA!
GILA MONSTERS DON'T SCARE ME EITHER!
GULP
TRY AGAIN!

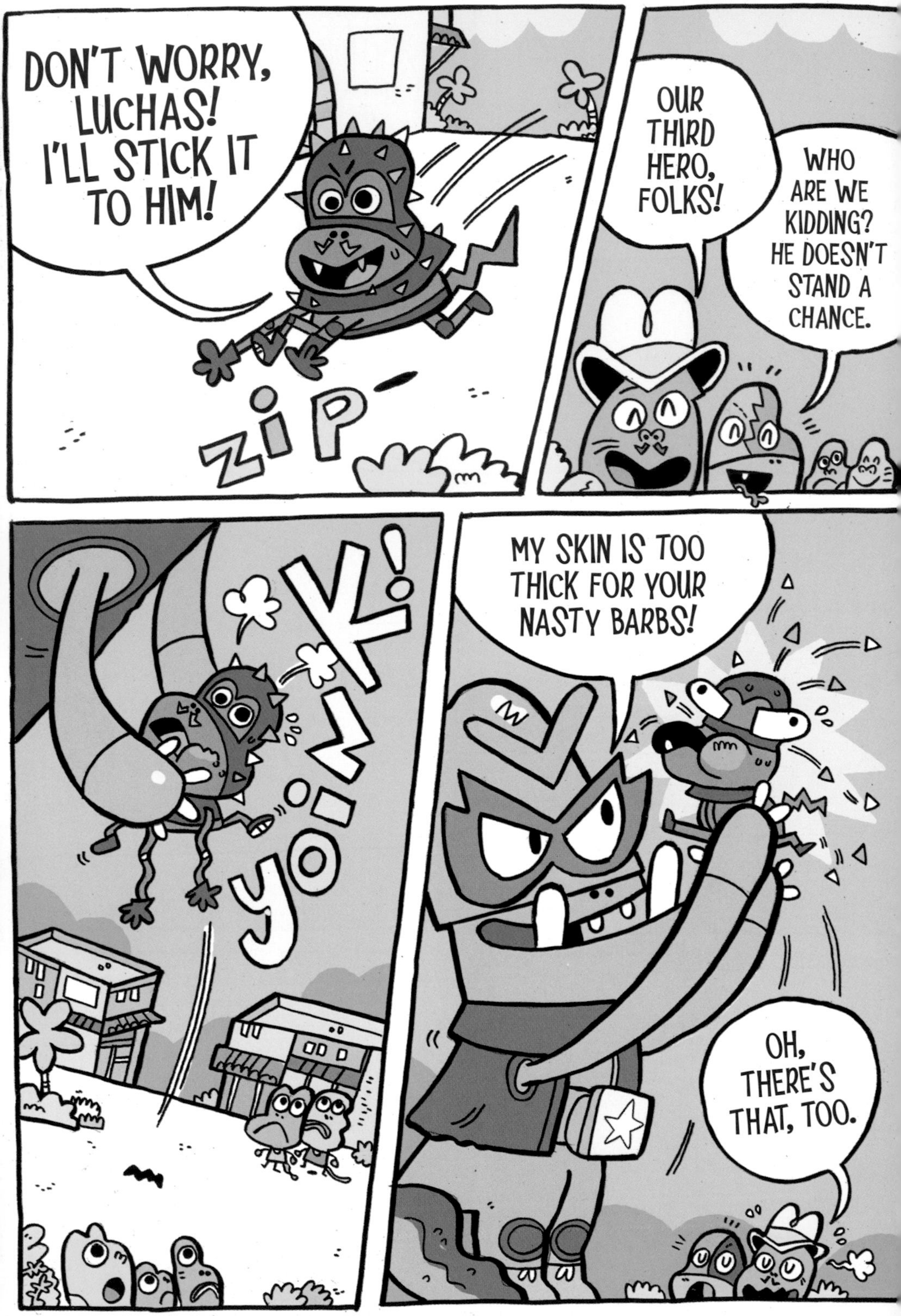
DON'T WORRY, LUCHAS! I'LL STICK IT TO HIM!
ZIP
OUR THIRD HERO, FOLKS!
WHO ARE WE KIDDING? HE DOESN'T STAND A CHANCE.
YOINK!
MY SKIN IS TOO THICK FOR YOUR NASTY BARBS!
OH, THERE'S THAT, TOO.

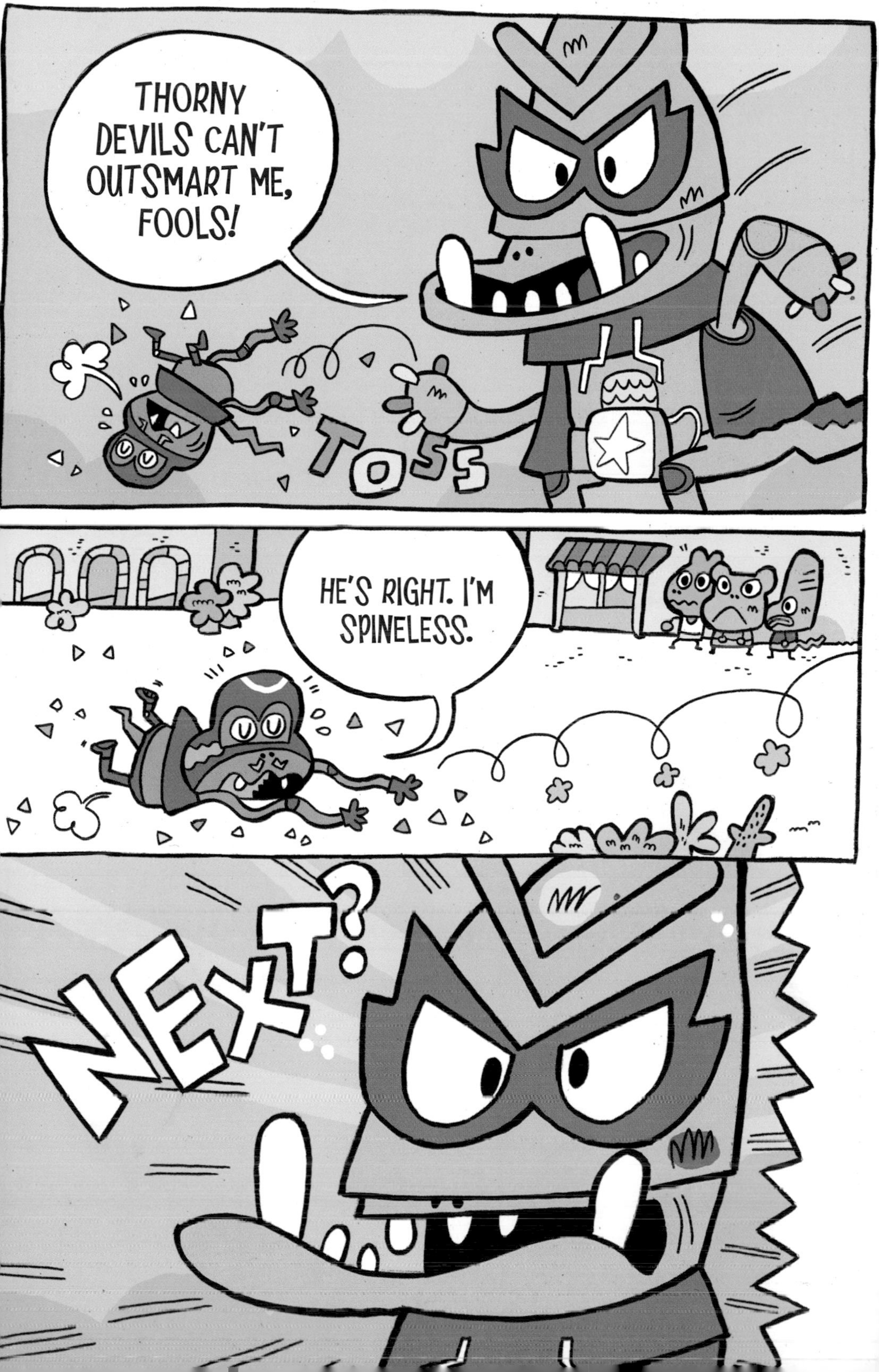
THORNY DEVILS CAN'T OUTSMART ME, FOOLS!
TOSS
HE'S RIGHT. I'M SPINELESS.
NEXT?

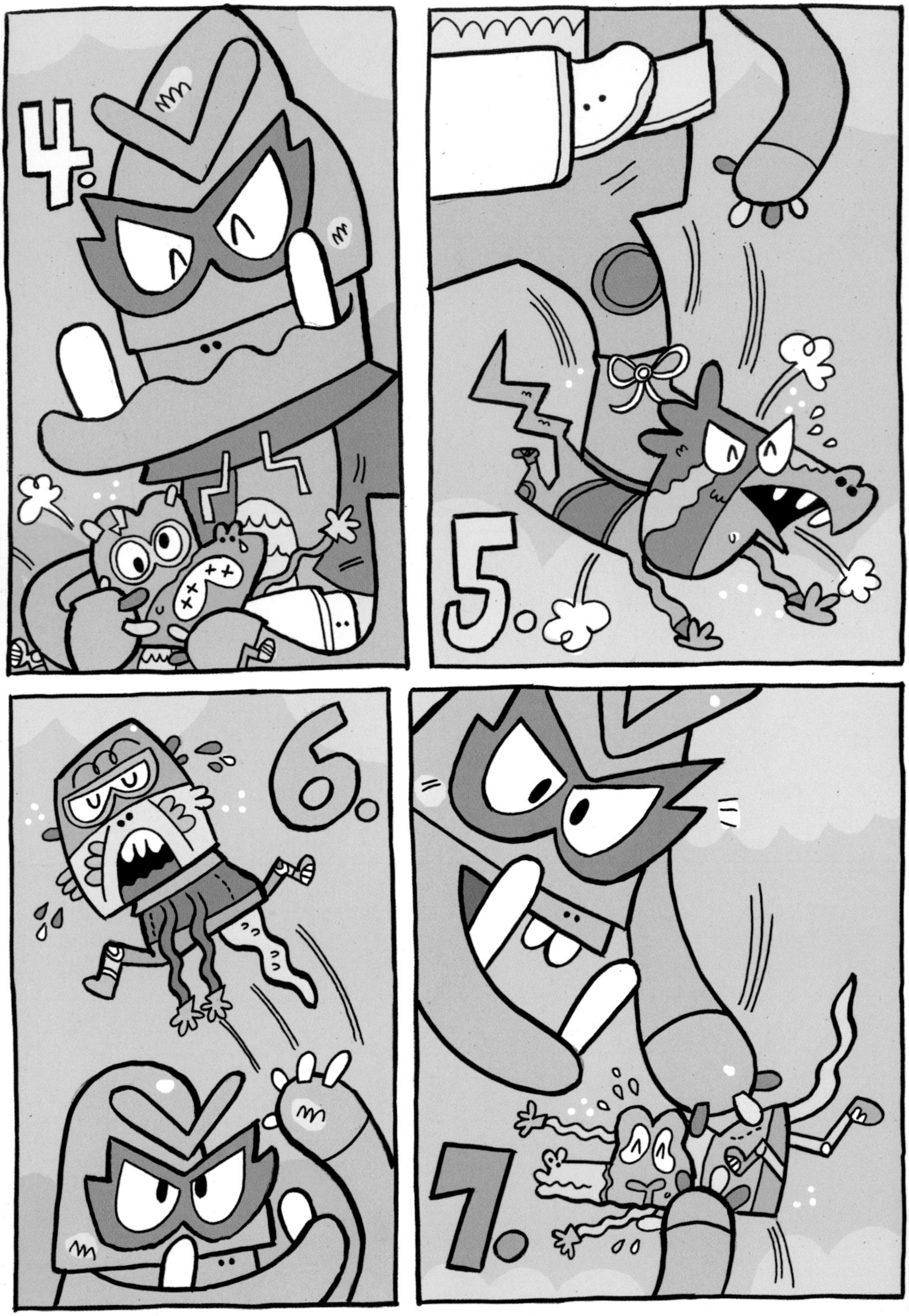
4.
5.
6.
7.

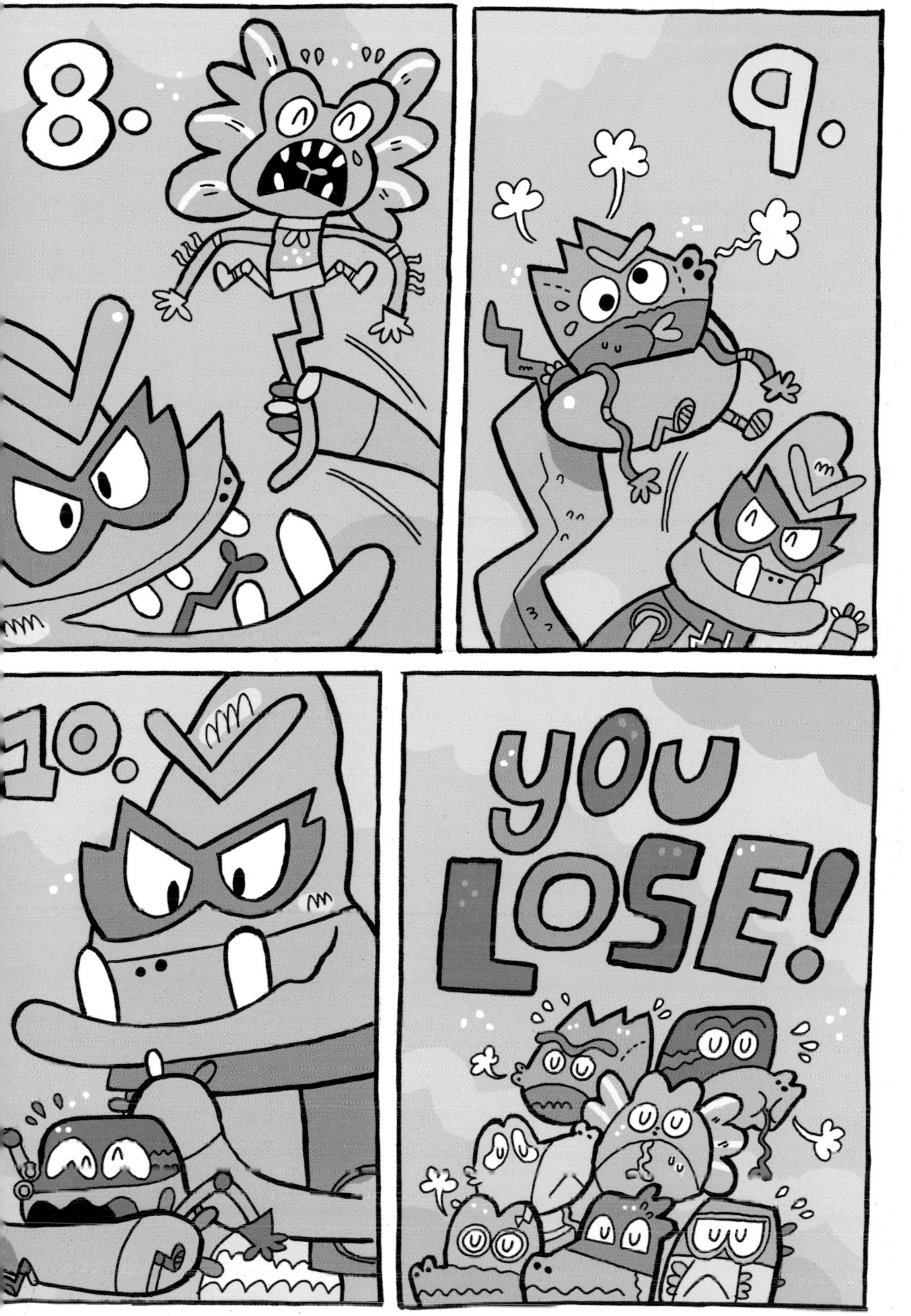
8.
9.
10.
YOU LOSE!

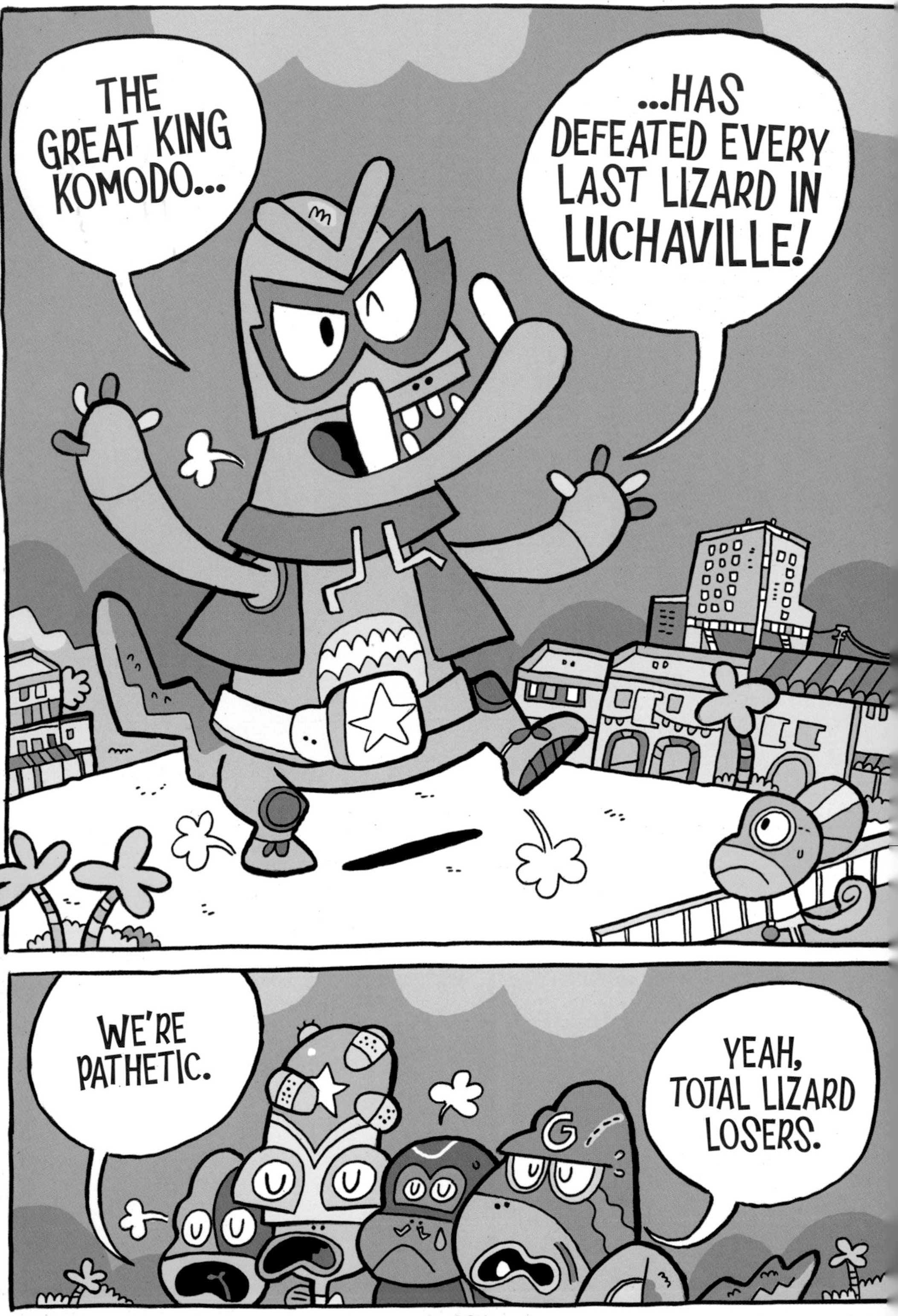
THE GREAT KING KOMODO...
...HAS DEFEATED EVERY LAST LIZARD IN LUCHAVILLE!
WE'RE PATHETIC.
YEAH, TOTAL LIZARD LOSERS.

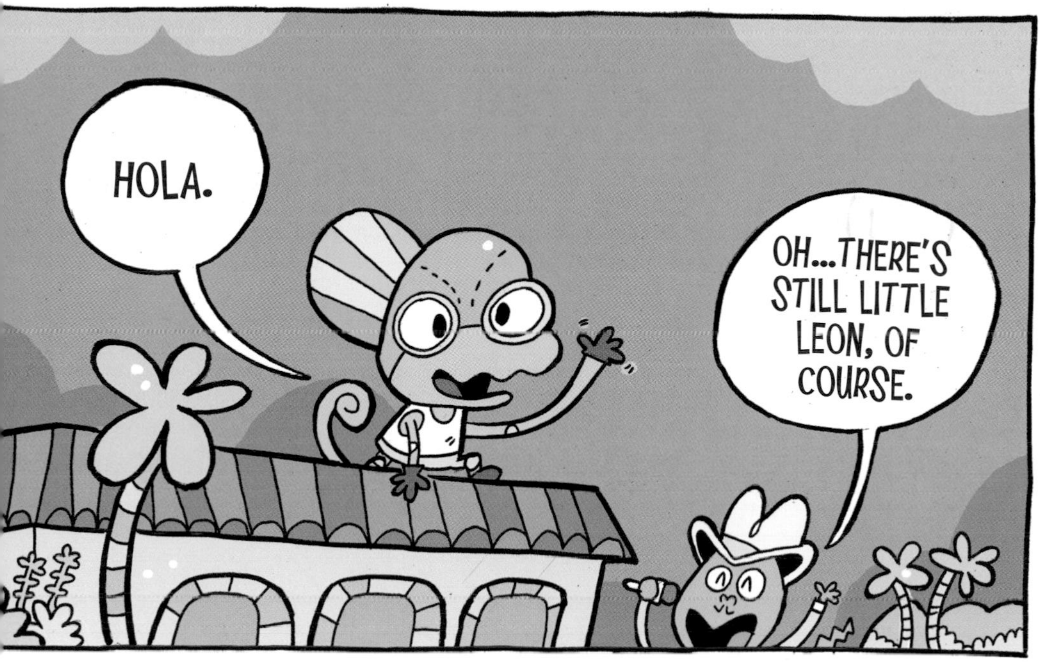
HOLA.
OH...THERE'S STILL LITTLE LEON, OF COURSE.

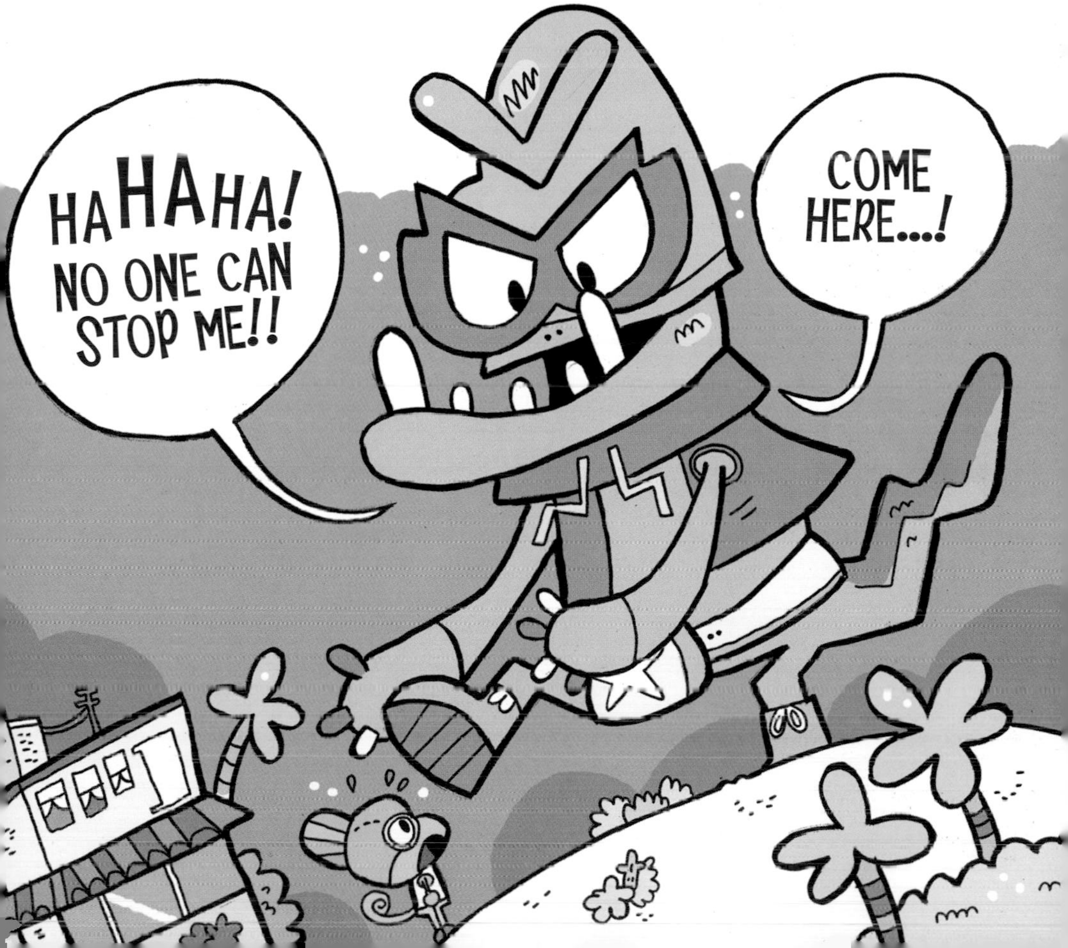
HAHAHA! NO ONE CAN STOP ME!!
COME HERE...!

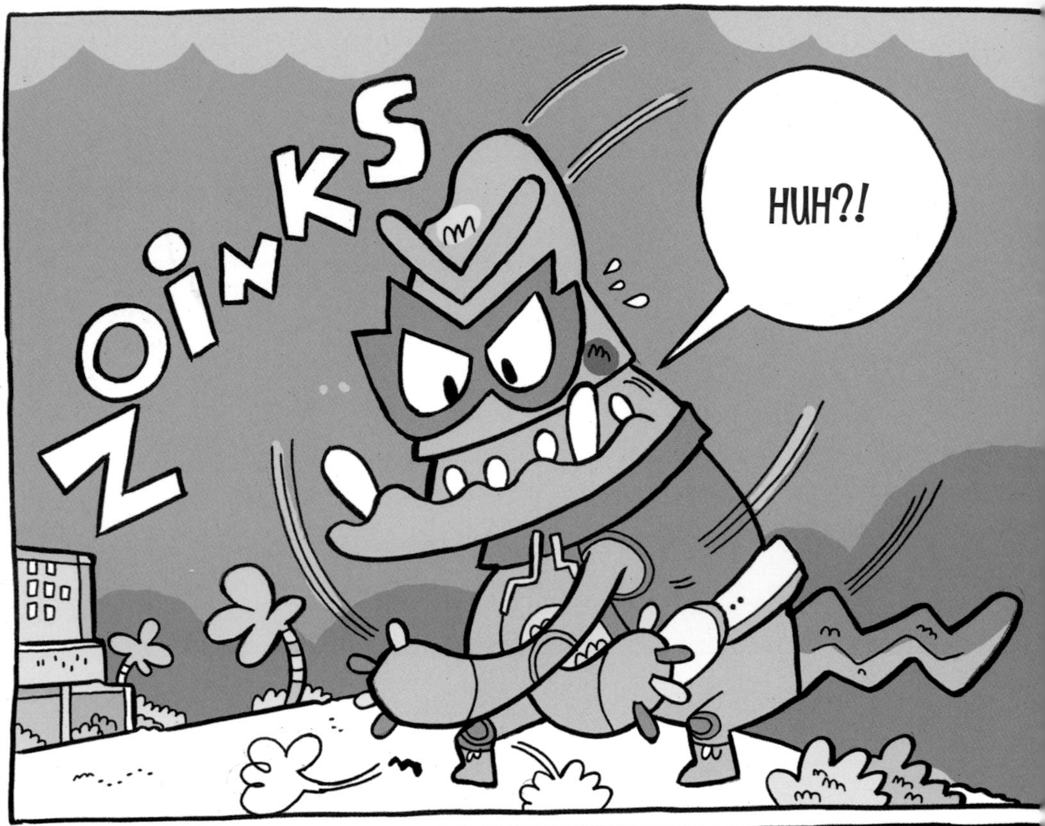
ZOINKS
HUH?!

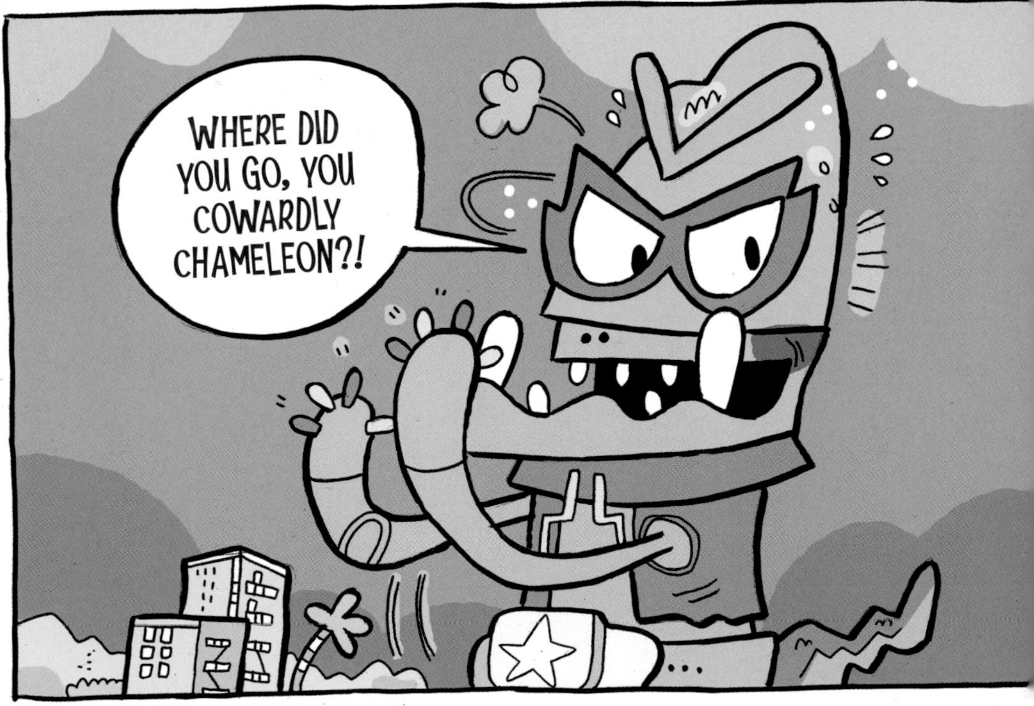
WHERE DID YOU GO, YOU COWARDLY CHAMELEON?!

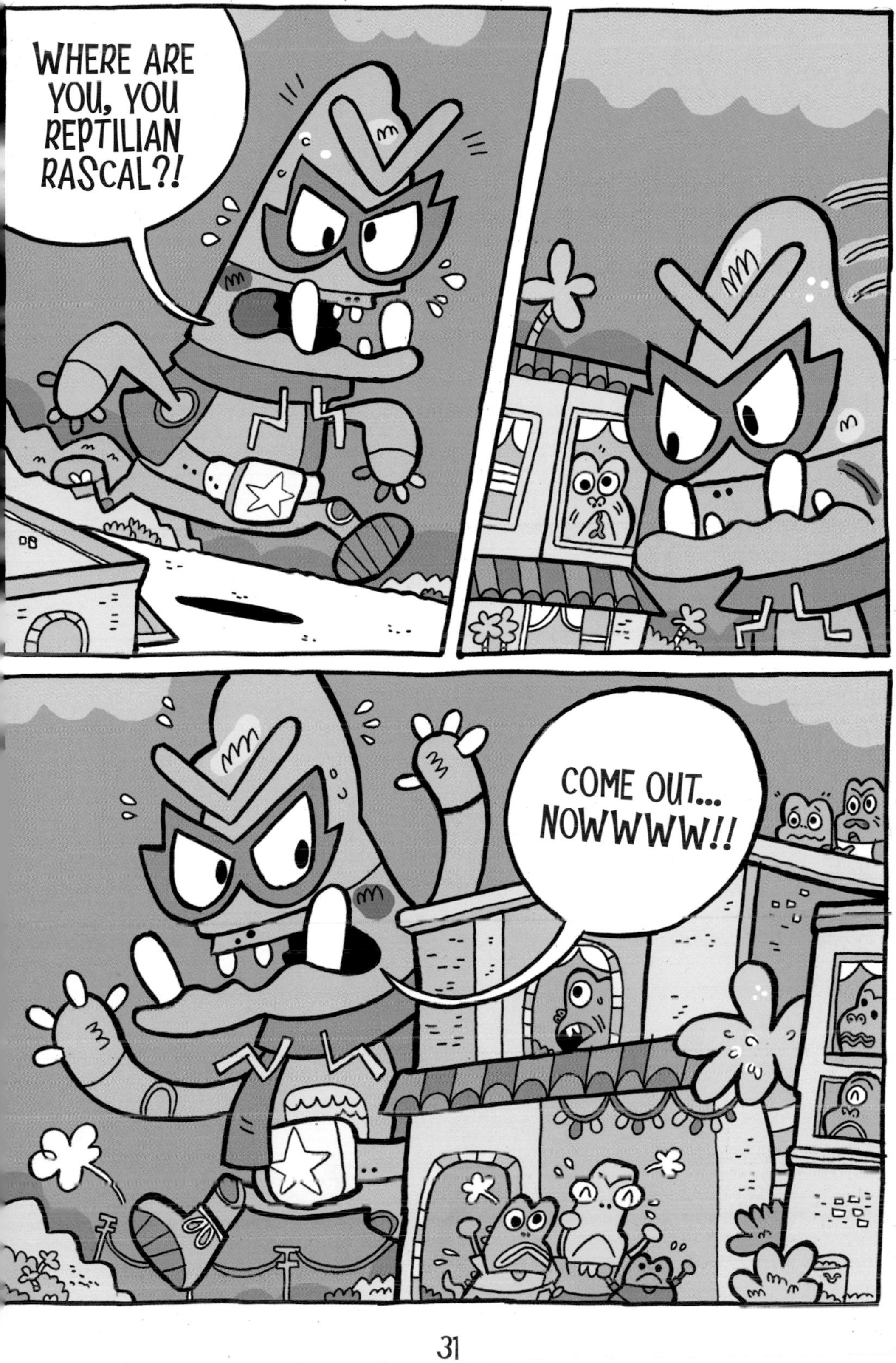
WHERE ARE YOU, YOU REPTILIAN RASCAL?!
COME OUT... NOWWWW!!

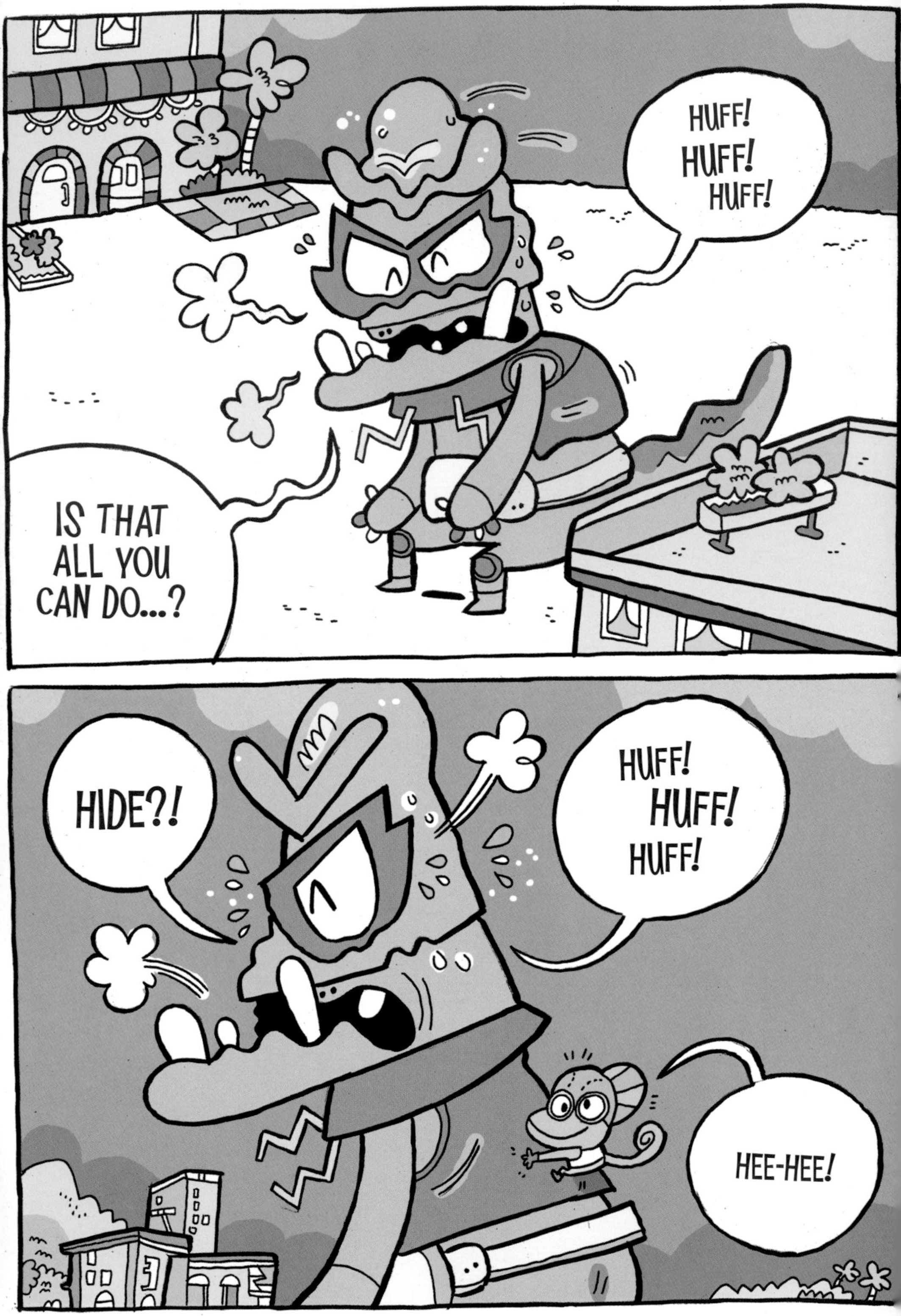
HUFF! HUFF! HUFF!
IS THAT ALL YOU CAN DO...?
HIDE?!
HUFF! HUFF! HUFF!
HEE-HEE!

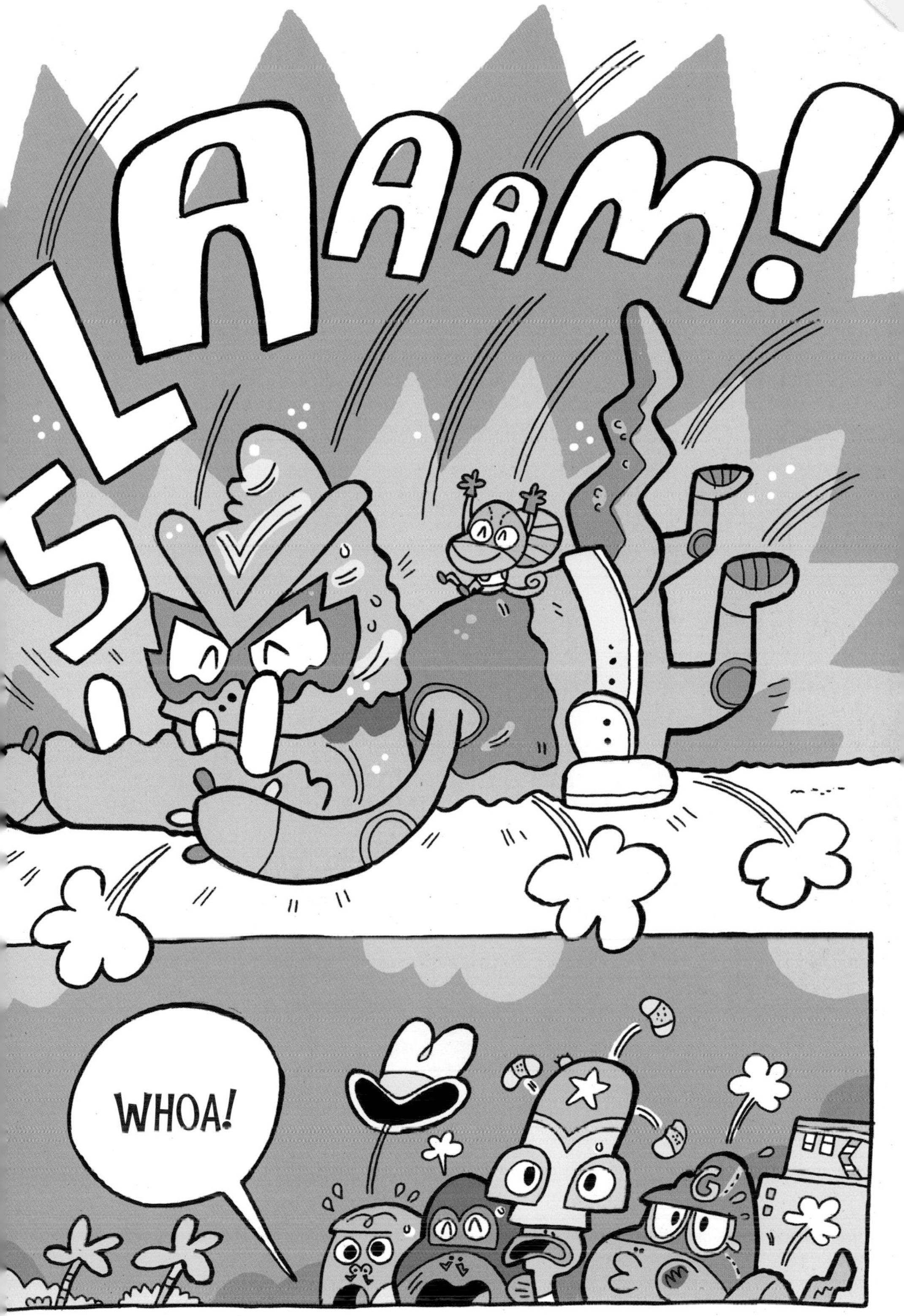
SLAAAAM!
WHOA!

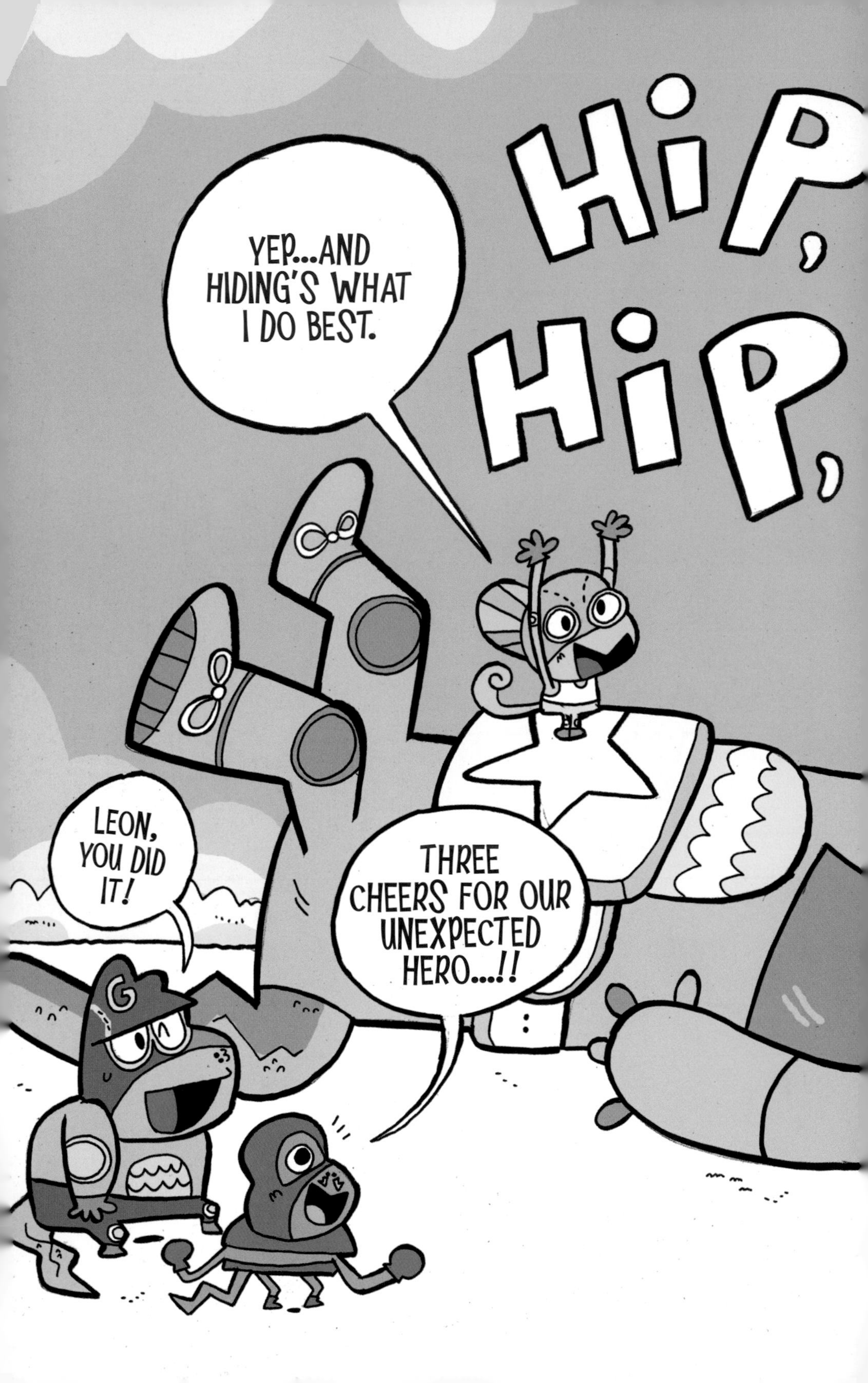
YEP...AND HIDING'S WHAT I DO BEST.
HIP, HIP,
LEON, YOU DID IT!
THREE CHEERS FOR OUR UNEXPECTED HERO...!!

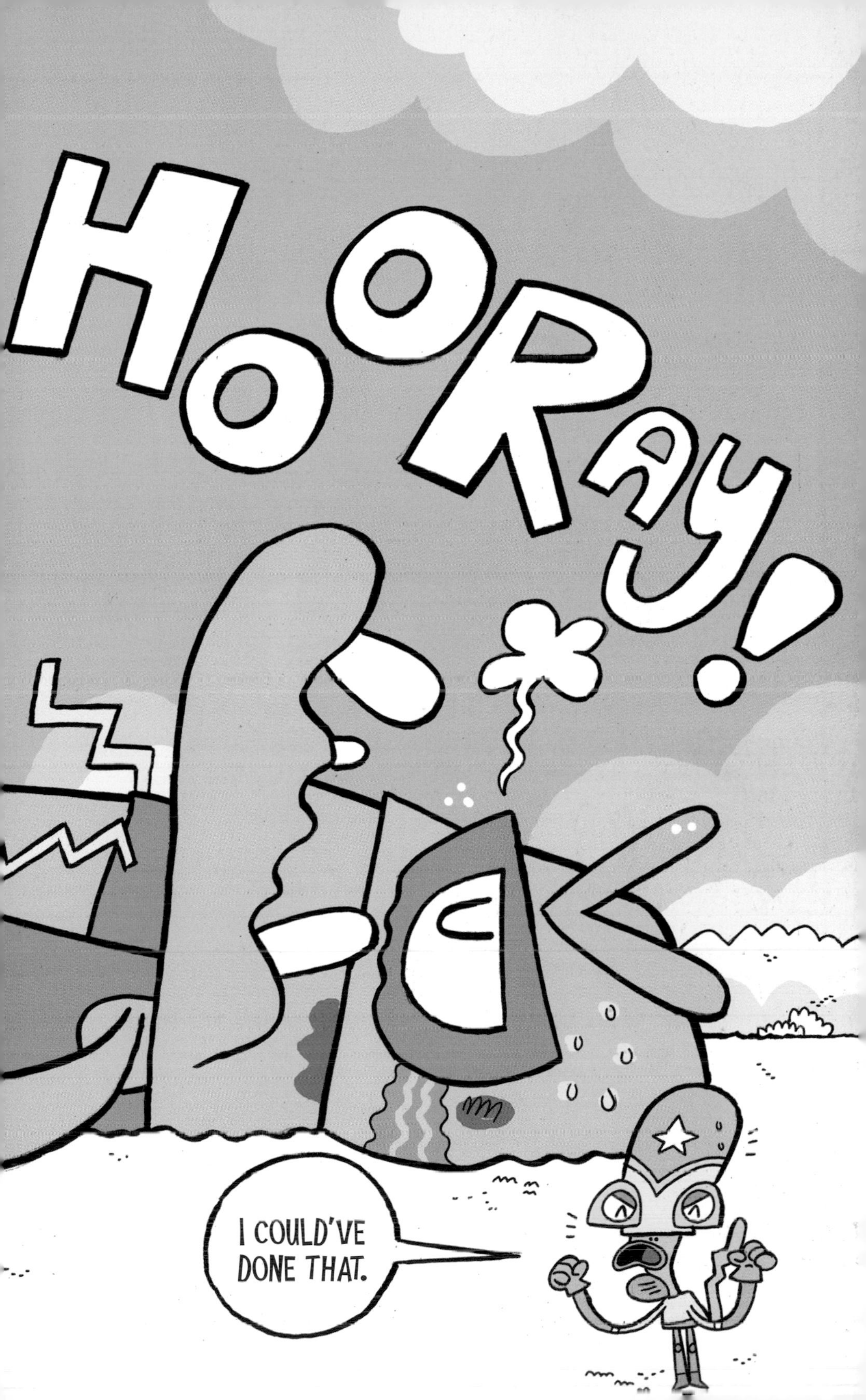
HOORAY!
I COULD'VE DONE THAT.

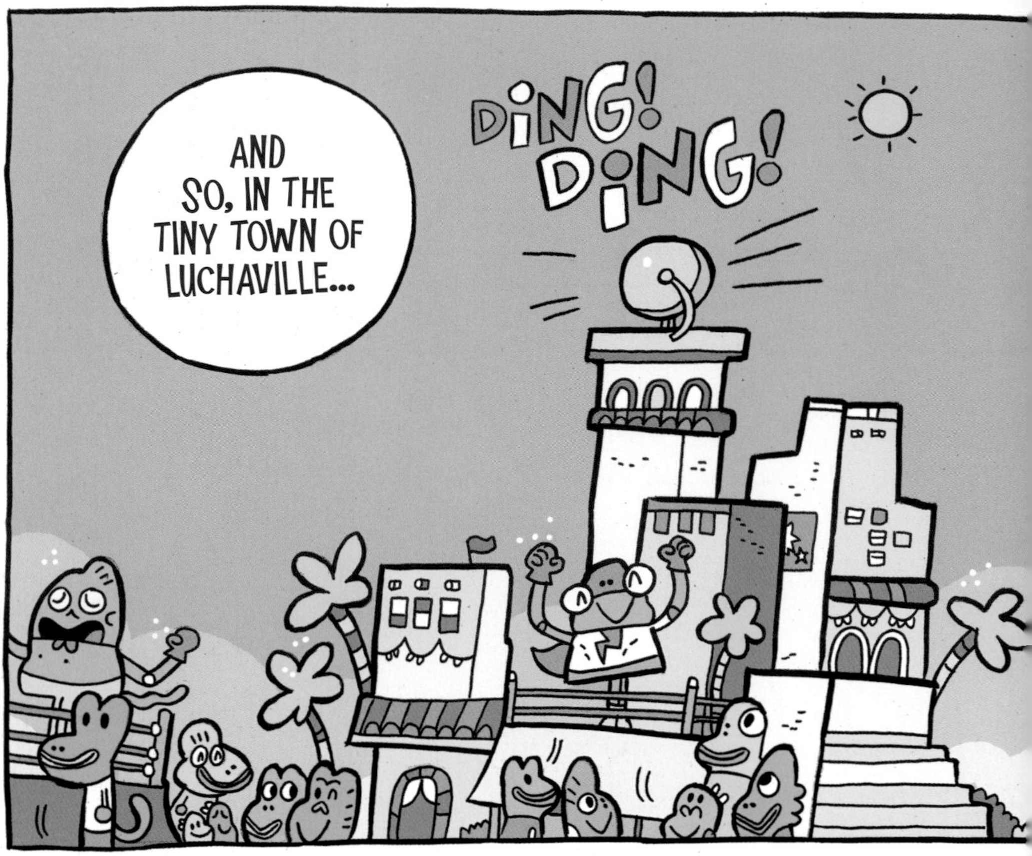
AND SO, IN THE TINY TOWN OF LUCHAVILLE...
DING! DING!

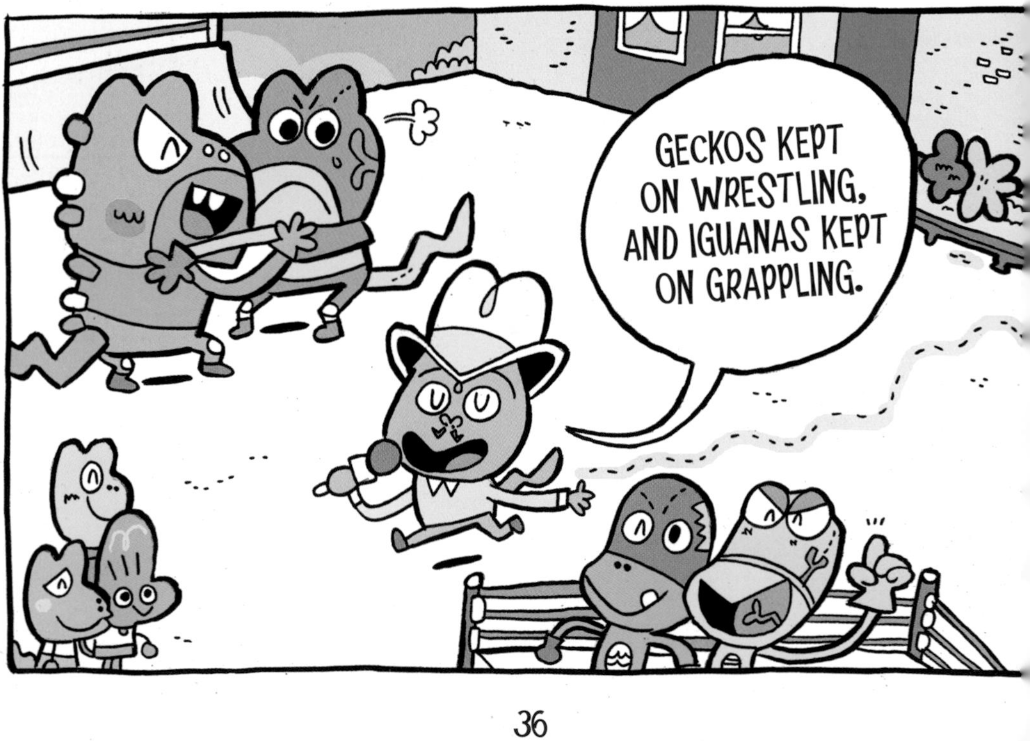
GECKOS KEPT ON WRESTLING, AND IGUANAS KEPT ON GRAPPLING.

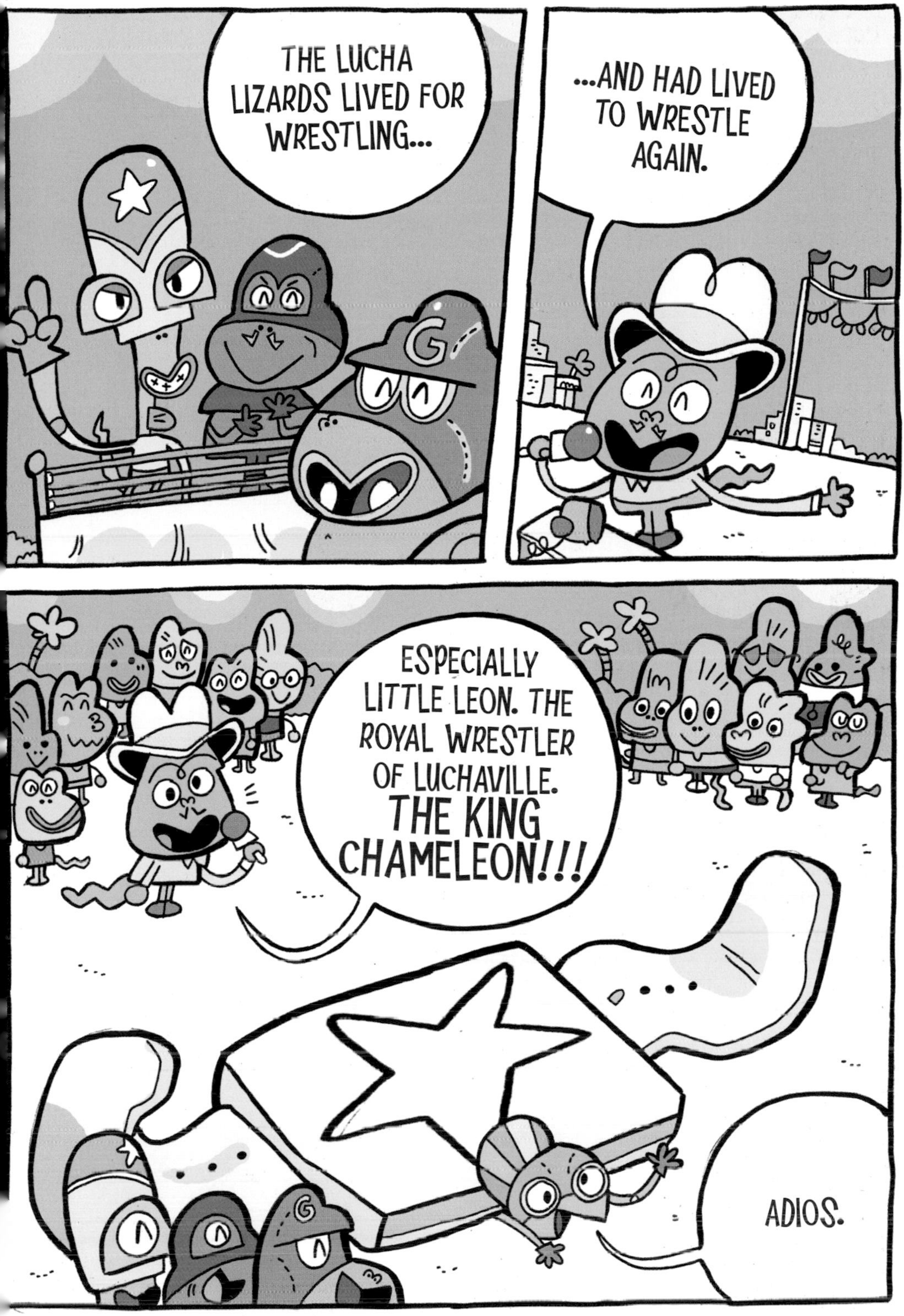
THE LUCHA LIZARDS LIVED FOR WRESTLING...
...AND HAD LIVED TO WRESTLE AGAIN.
ESPECIALLY LITTLE LEON. THE ROYAL WRESTLER OF LUCHAVILLE. THE KING CHAMELEON!!!
...
...
ADIOS.

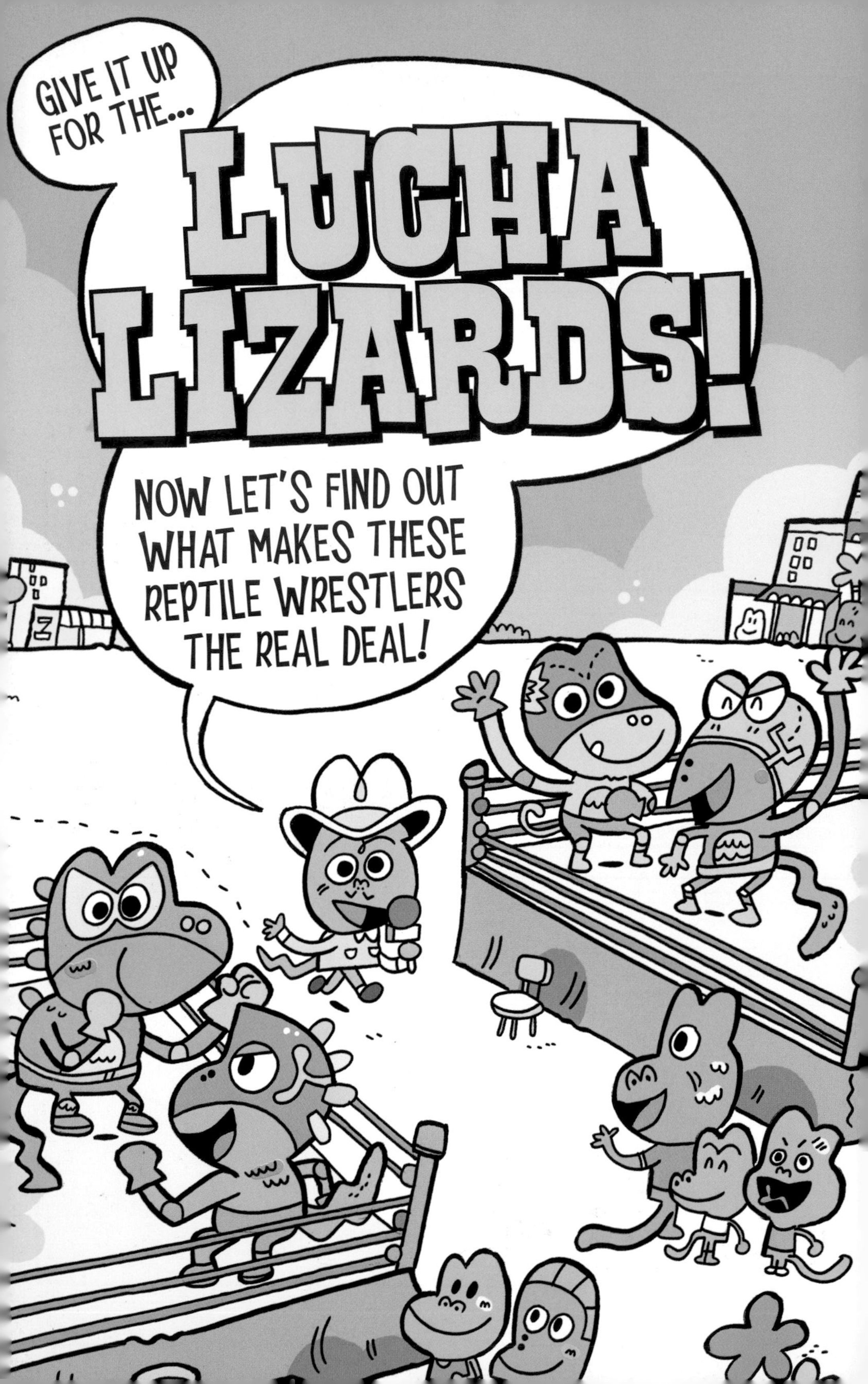
GIVE IT UP FOR THE...
LUCHA LIZARDS!
NOW LET'S FIND OUT WHAT MAKES THESE REPTILE WRESTLERS THE REAL DEAL!

GREEN SALAMANDERS

REAL NAME: *ANEIDES AENEUS*
WEIGHT: *6 OUNCES*
LENGTH: *4 INCHES*
HABITAT: *HARDWOOD FOREST*

POWERGRID	1	2	3	4	5
STRENGTH:	*	*	*		
SKILL:	*	*	*		
SMARTS:	*				

BIO: PERHAPS ASHAMED THAT THEY ARE AMPHIBIANS NOT LIZARDS, GREEN SALAMANDERS ARE RARELY SEEN IN THEIR APPALACHIAN MOUNTAIN HOME.

SPECIAL MOVES:
THE TAIL WHIP!
THE SLIME TIME!!
THE AMPHIBIAN ATTACK!!!

BLUE-TONGUED SKINKS

REAL NAME: *TILIQUA SCINCOIDES*
WEIGHT: *15 OUNCES*
LENGTH: *23 INCHES*
HABITAT: *GRASSLAND, RAINFOREST, DESERT*

BIO: THESE AWESOME AUSSIES ARE FRIENDS, NOT FIGHTERS. BUT THEY'RE NOT AFRAID TO GIVE COMPETITORS A GOOD (BLUE) TONGUE LASHING.

POWERGRID	1	2	3	4	5
STRENGTH:	*	*			
SKILL:	*	*	*		
SMARTS:	*	*			

SPECIAL MOVE:
THE TONGUE TWISTER!

FLYING DRAGON

REAL NAME: *DRACO VOLANS*
WEIGHT: *1 OUNCE*
LENGTH: *8 INCHES*
HABITAT: *RAINFOREST*

BIO: NEW TO REPTILE WRESTLING, THE SKY'S THE LIMIT FOR THIS GIFTED GLIDER FROM SOUTHEAST ASIA.

POWERGRID	1	2	3	4	5
STRENGTH:	*				
SKILL:	*	*	*	*	*
SMARTS:	*	*	*		

SPECIAL MOVES: THE LEAPIN' LIZARD & THE FLYING DROPKICK!

THORNY DEVIL

REAL NAME: *MOLOCH HORRIDUS*
WEIGHT: *3 OUNCES*
LENGTH: *8 INCHES*
HABITAT: *DESERT*

BIO: HAILING FROM AUSTRALIA, THIS LIL' DEVIL IS ANYTHING BUT DULL. WITH SHARP SPINES AND A FALSE FACE ON HIS BACK, HE IS TRULY A MASTER OF DEFENSE.

POWERGRID	1	2	3	4	5
STRENGTH:	*	*	*		
SKILL:	*	*	*		
SMARTS:	*	*	*		

SPECIAL MOVES:
THE CACTUS CLOTHESLINE!
THE FAKE FACE FREAKOUT!

GILA MONSTER

REAL NAME: *HELODERMA SUSPECTUM*
WEIGHT: *3 POUNDS*
LENGTH: *2 FEET*
HABITAT: *DESERT*

POWERGRID	1	2	3	4	5
STRENGTH:	*	*	*	*	
SKILL:	*	*			
SMARTS:	*				

BIO: THIS DESERT DEMON SPITS A REIGN OF TERROR THROUGHOUT NORTHWESTERN MEXICO AND THE SOUTHWESTERN UNITED STATES. AS ONE OF ONLY TWO VENOMOUS LIZARDS IN THE WORLD, THE GILA MONSTER IS A DEADLY OPPONENT!

FACT: THE GILA MONSTER IS THE LARGEST LIZARD NATIVE TO THE UNITED STATES!

SPECIAL MOVES:
THE MONSTER MASH!
THE LIZARD LICK!!
THE BEHEMOTH BITE!!!

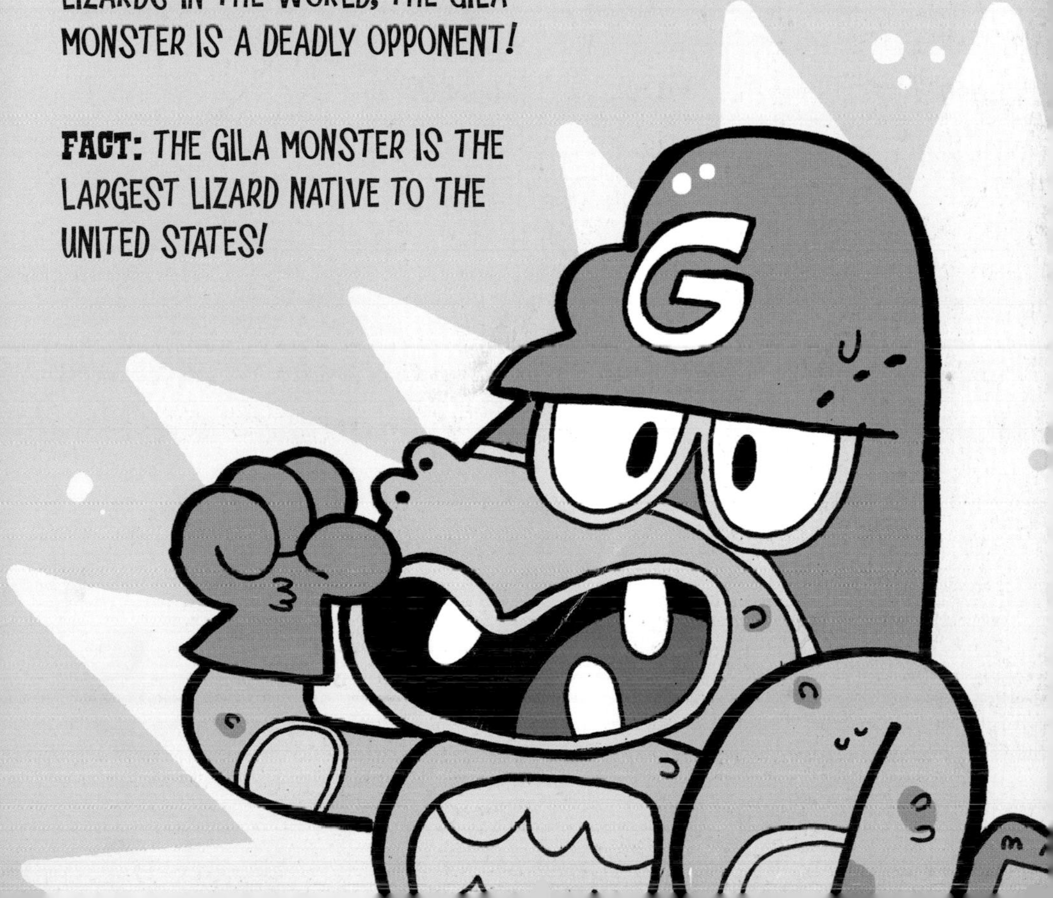
G

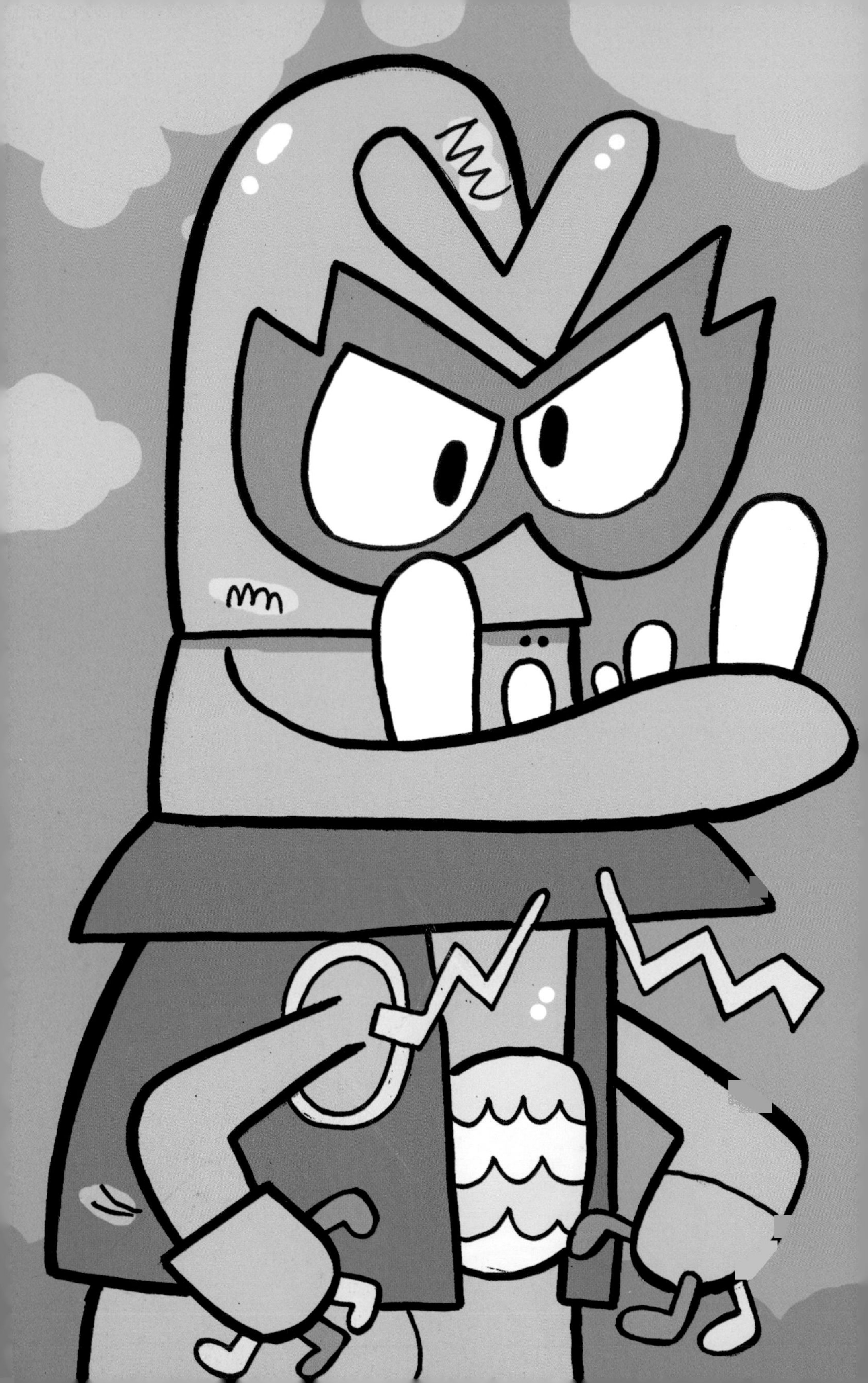

KING KOMODO

REAL NAME: *VARANUS KOMODOENSIS*
WEIGHT: *176 POUNDS!*
LENGTH: *10 FEET!*
HABITAT: *GRASSLAND & TROPICAL FOREST*

POWERGRID	1	2	3	4	5
STRENGTH:	*	*	*	*	*
SKILL:	*				
SMARTS:	*	*			

BIO: FROM THE ISLANDS OF INDONESIA COMES THE LARGEST LIZARD ON EARTH...THE KOMODO DRAGON. WITH ROW UPON ROW OF RAZOR-SHARP TEETH, THIS BEHEMOTH WAS KING OF THE LIZARD WORLD AND UNMATCHED IN THE LIZARD WRESTLING ASSOCIATION...UNTIL NOW.

SPECIAL MOVES:
THE DRAGON WHIP!
THE ROYAL RUMBLE!!
THE KOMODO KICK!!!

FACT: KOMODO DRAGON SALIVA CONTAINS MORE THAN 50 STRAINS OF BACTERIA, WHICH CAN KILL AN OPPONENT BY BLOOD POISONING!

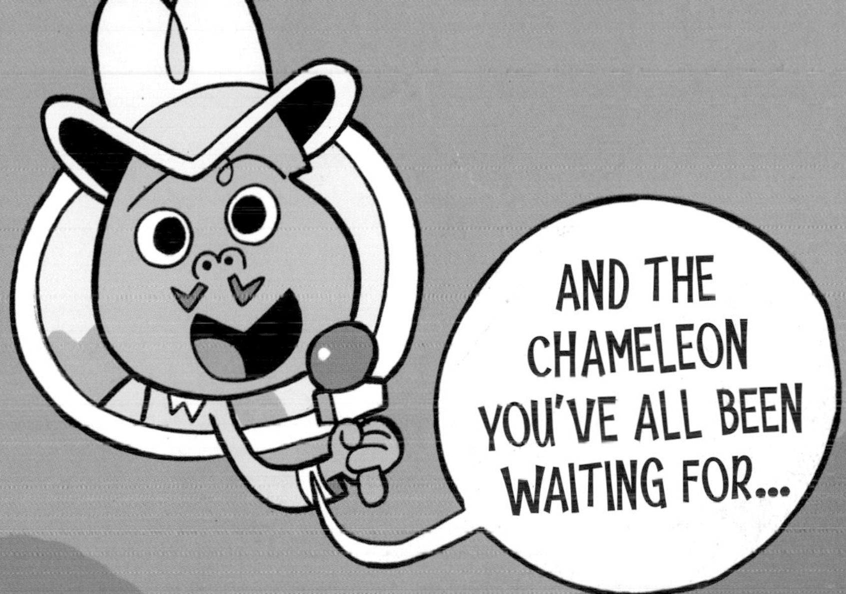
AND THE CHAMELEON YOU'VE ALL BEEN WAITING FOR...

LITTLE LEON

REAL NAME: *CHAMAELEO CALYPTRATUS*
WEIGHT: *7 OUNCES*
LENGTH: *15 INCHES*
HABITAT: *DRY PLATEAU, MOUNTAIN, & RIVER VALLEY*

POWERGRID	1	2	3	4	5
STRENGTH:	*				
SKILL:	*	*	*	*	*
SMARTS:	*	*	*	*	*

BIO: THIS MOUNTAINOUS TREE DWELLER IS A MASTER OF DISGUISE, ABLE TO CHANGE COLORS IN THE BLINK OF A GOOGLY EYE!

FACT: LITTLE LEON HAS EYES THAT CAN MOVE INDEPENDENTLY AND LOOK IN TWO DIRECTIONS AT ONCE, AS WELL AS SWIVEL NEARLY 180 DEGREES!

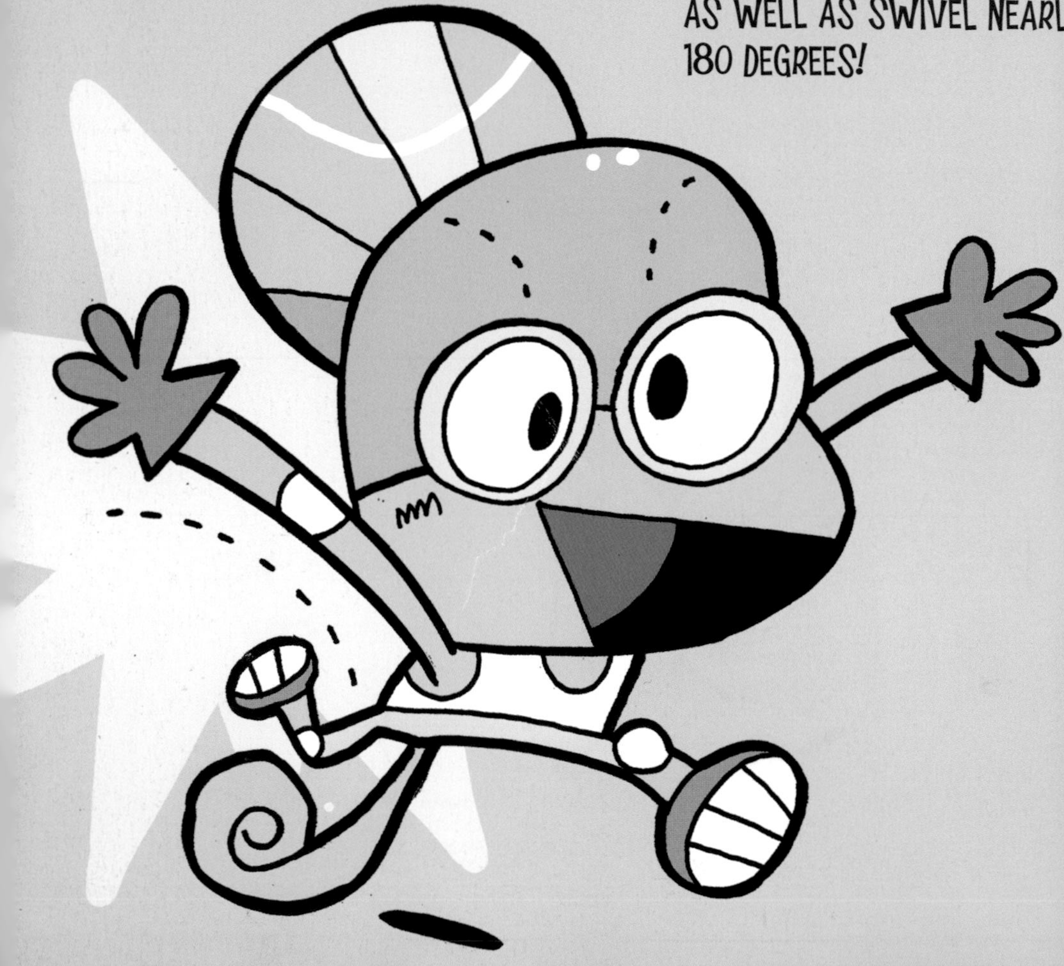

SPECIAL MOVES:

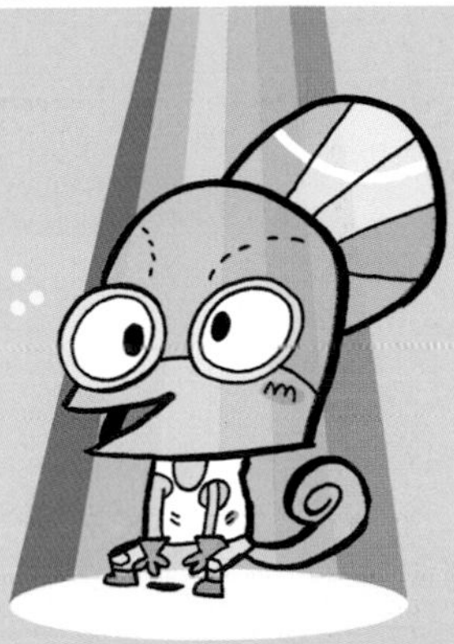

THE RAINBOW CONNECTION!

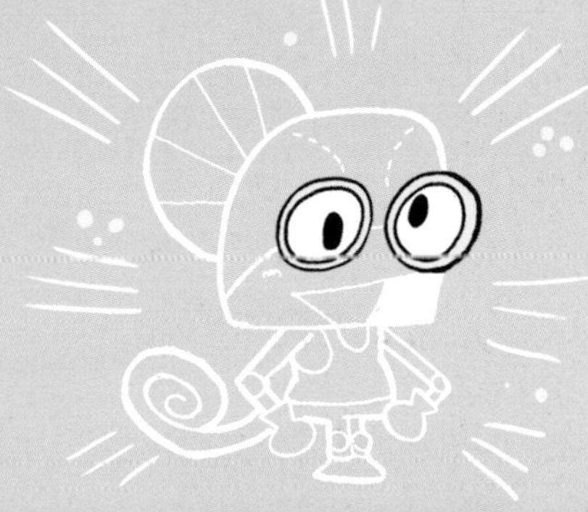

THE INVISILIZARD!

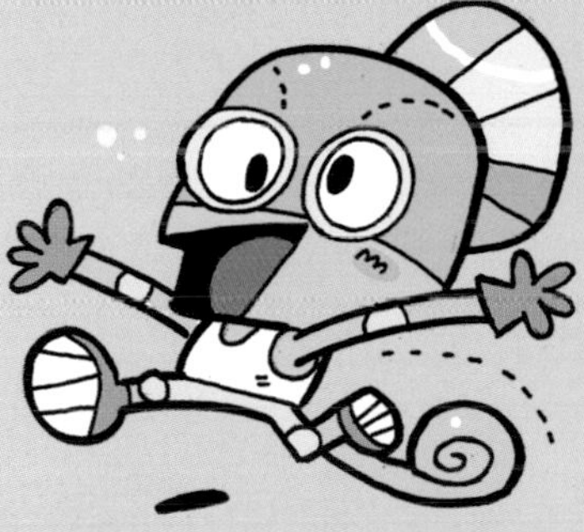

THE RUNAROUND!

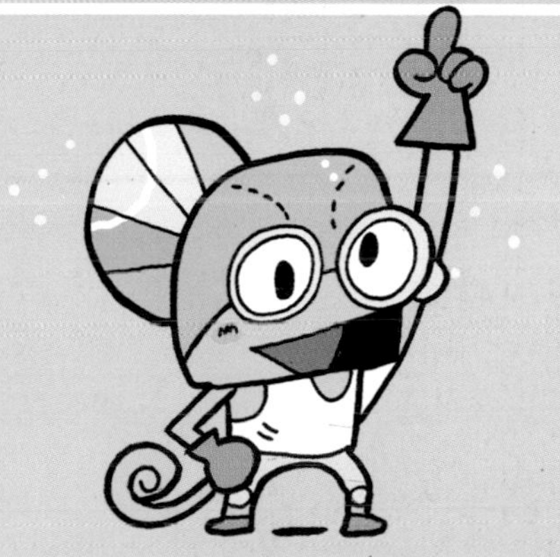

THE DISCO DAZZLER!

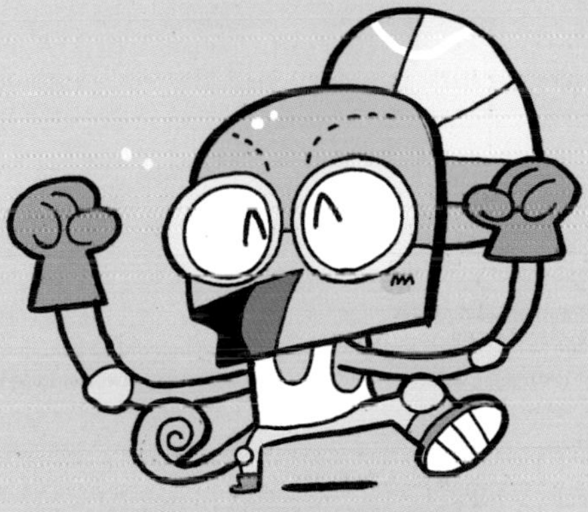

THE HAPPY DANCE!

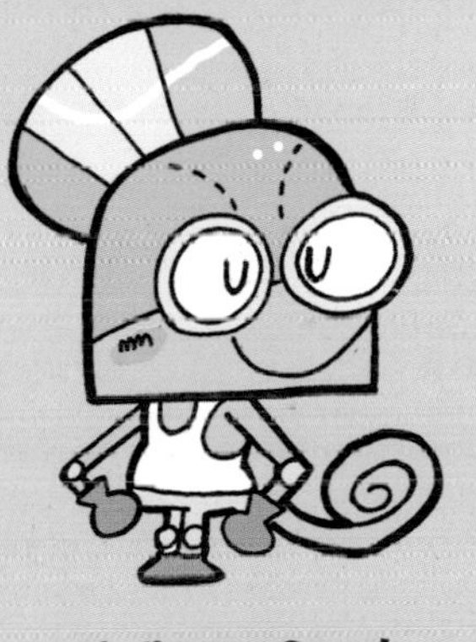

EL PROFESOR!

THE LWA

THE LIZARD WRESTLING ASSOCIATION, ALSO KNOWN AS THE LWA, WAS ESTABLISHED IN 1933 BY A BUNCH OF REPTILES WHO WANTED TO RUMBLE. SINCE THEN, REAL-LIFE LIZARDS HAVE BATTLED TOOTH AND TAIL FOR THE COVETED ONE-STAR BELT AND THE TITLE OF KING LIZARD!!

HOW TO SPEAK LUCHA

(OTHERWISE KNOWN AS SPANISH)

ADIOS (ah-dee-OHS)--goodbye or so long

AMIGOS (uh-MEE-gohs)--friends, pals, or besties!

COLORES (kuh-LOHR-ehs)--colors, like a rainbow

HOLA (OH-Lah)--hello

LOCO (LOH-koh)--crazy, or out of your mind

LUCHA (LOO-cha)--wrestling

MUCHOS (MOO-chos)--many

Si (SEE)--yes

CREATORS

DONALD LEMKE

THIS GUY WORKS AS A CHILDREN'S BOOK EDITOR! HE HAS WRITTEN DOZENS OF ALL-AGE COMICS AND CHILDREN'S BOOKS FOR CAPSTONE, HARPERCOLLINS, RUNNING PRESS, AND MORE. DONALD LIVES IN MINNESOTA WITH HIS BEAUTIFUL WIFE, AMY, THEIR NOT-SO-GOLDEN RETRIEVER, PAULIE, AND A BLACK CAT NAMED DYLAN.

CHRIS ELIOPOULOS

THIS GUY IS A PROFESSIONAL ILLUSTRATOR AND CARTOONIST FROM CHICAGO! HE IS ALSO AN ADJUNCT PROFESSOR AT COLUMBIA COLLEGE CHICAGO IN THE ART AND DESIGN DEPARTMENT. HE IS THE WRITER AND ARTIST ON SEVERAL ALL-AGES GRAPHIC NOVELS AND SERIES: "OKIE DOKIE DONUTS" PUBLISHED BY TOP SHELF; "GABBA BALL!" PUBLISHED BY ONI PRESS; AND "MONSTER PARTY" PUBLISHED BY KOYAMA PRESS. OTHER CLIENTS INCLUDE DISNEY ANIMATION STUDIOS, YO GABBA GABBA!, NICK JR., CLOUDKID, AND SIMON AND SCHUSTER.

THE LUCHA FUN DOESN'T STOP HERE!

DISCOVER MORE AT...

WWW.CAPSTONEKIDS.COM

FIND COOL WEBSITES AND MORE BOOKS LIKE THIS ONE AT **WWW.FACTHOUND.COM**

JUST TYPE IN THE BOOK ID: **9781434232854** AND YOU'RE READY TO GO!

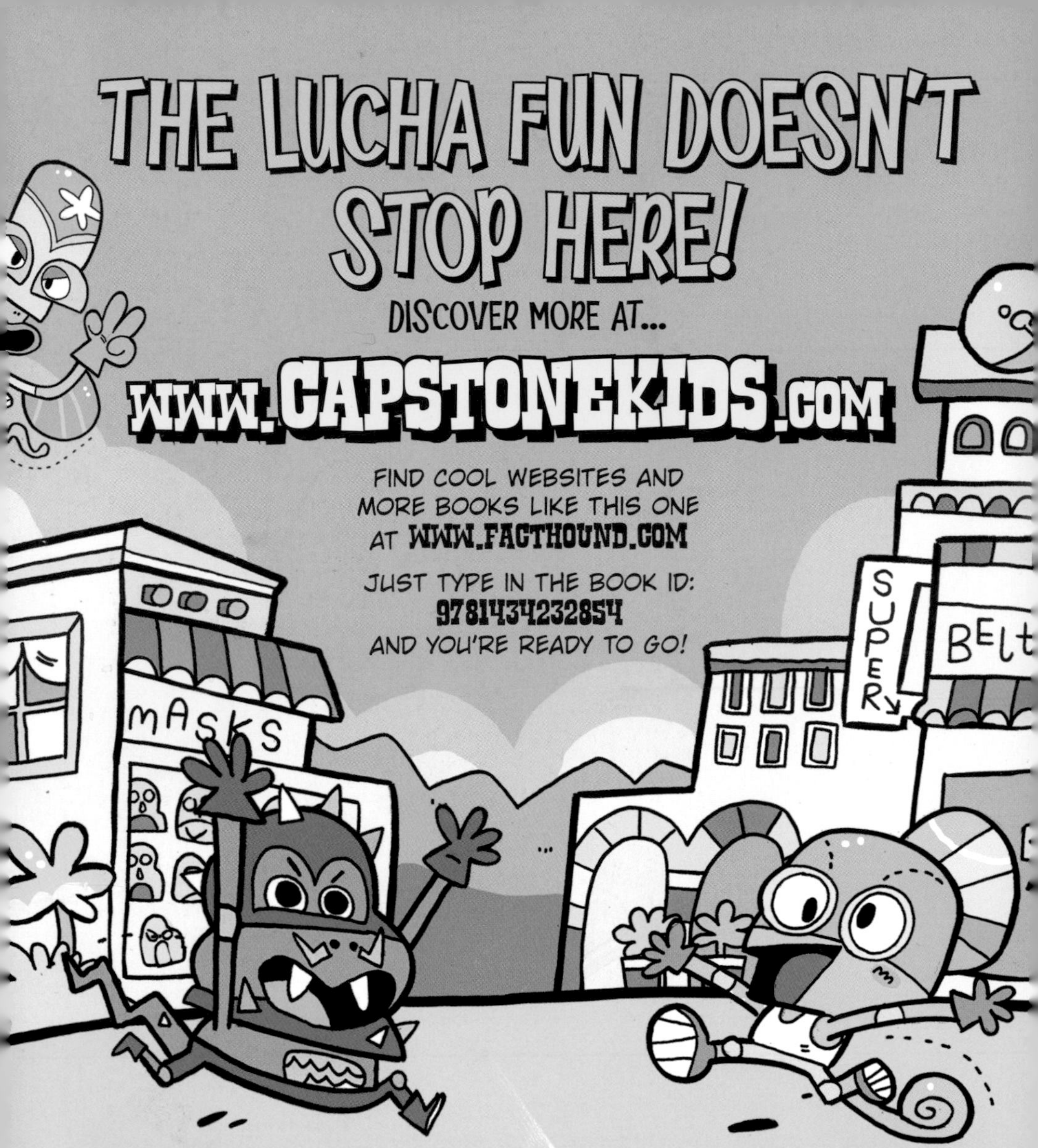

mASKS
SUPER
BElt

ASHLEY C. ANDERSEN ZANTOP - *PUBLISHER*
MICHAEL DAHL - *EDITORIAL DIRECTOR*
HEATHER KINDSETH - *CREATIVE DIRECTOR*
BOB LENTZ - *ART DIRECTOR*
BRANN GARVEY - *SENIOR DESIGNER*

STONE ARCH BOOKS
1710 ROE CREST DRIVE,
NORTH MANKATO, MINNESOTA 56003
WWW.CAPSTONEPUB.COM

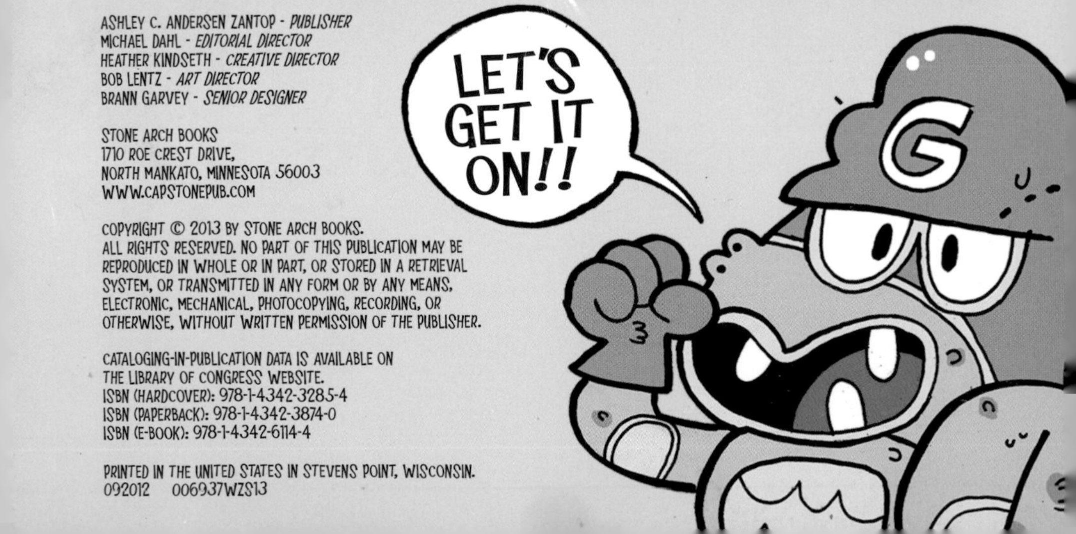

LET'S GET IT ON!!

CATALOGING-IN-PUBLICATION DATA IS AVAILABLE ON THE LIBRARY OF CONGRESS WEBSITE.
ISBN (HARDCOVER): 978-1-4342-3285-4
ISBN (PAPERBACK): 978-1-4342-3874-0
ISBN (E-BOOK): 978-1-4342-6114-4

PRINTED IN THE UNITED STATES IN STEVENS POINT, WISCONSIN.
092012 006937WZS13